Jammy Dodgers on the Run

BOWERING SIVERS

MACMILLAN CHILDREN'S BOOKS

First published 2004 by Macmillan Children's Books

This edition published 2005 by Macmillan Children's Books
a division of Macmillan Publishers Limited
20 New Wharf Road, London N1 9RR
Basingstoke and Oxford
www.panmacmillan.com

Associated companies throughout the world

ISBN 0 330 43663 5

3 5 7 9 8 6 4 2

A CIP catalogue record for this book is available from
the British Library.

Typeset by Intype Libra Ltd
Printed and bound in Great Britain by Mackays of Chatham plc, Kent

*To Edie and Jack with thanks for their love
and support when I needed it most*

Acknowledgements

I am very grateful to Brian Keaney for pointing me in the right direction, to Pat White for rescuing me from the wilderness, to Polly Nolan and Penny Morris for their plummy suggestions, and to Sarah Dudman for being a splendiferous editor.

When writing *Jammy Dodgers on the Run* I read many books to make sure I was painting an accurate picture of Victorian London. By far the most valuable to me were the works of Henry Mayhew, a gifted journalist who had the courage to go into the dreadful 'rookeries' and record all that he heard and saw there with compassion and an extraordinary attention to detail. Kellow Chesney's *Victorian Underworld* was also an excellent source of information. And then there's my *Slang Dictionary*, which was published in 1873 by Chatto and Windus. I have used it and loved it to bits. When the last yellowing page fluttered to the floor I took my dictionary to a bookbinder, who put it together again. In a few years, of course, I shall have loved it to bits yet again . . . Still, it keeps the bookbinders in business, doesn't it?

Bowering Sivers was born in Middlesex and grew up in Wembley Park, within the sound of the stadium on Cup Final day. Her family comes from a long line of Londoners. There were members of the Sivers family living in Southwark at the same time as Shakespeare. They worked as 'watermen' – providing a sixteenth-century taxicab service on the River Thames.

After graduating from the University of Southampton, Bowering Sivers took a job teaching French in Zambia – and got bitten by the travel bug. She has worked in Kenya and across Canada, and once spent a year touring Europe in a caravan. Married to a photographer, she can now be found living happily by the sea and taking her dogs for walks along the beach. Unless that travel-bug bite starts itching again . . .

Praise for *Jammy Dodgers on the Run*

'One of our fave reads. There's heaps of scary stuff – wicked!'
K-club magazine

'Do not miss this chance to read a truly brilliant book. If I had to give a mark out of a hundred, this book would be a hundred and ten!'
William Howarth, aged 10

Also by Bowering Sivers

Jammy Dodgers Go Underground

Contents

1

Jem was trying to pluck the chicken that his grandmother had killed that morning, but he had a feeling the old lady hadn't done the job properly, because every time he grabbed a feather and tugged, the angry bird let out a squawk and pecked him.

'I keep tellin' Gran you can't kill a chicken by puttin' a spell on it,' he complained, sucking his bruised fingers. 'You got to cut its head off with a chopper.'

'Gran's spells never work, anyway,' said Ned. 'Remember when I had them warts? Littl'uns, they were. Then she rubbed one of her magic potions on them and the next day I'd got warts all over me, big as gooseberries. I still got one on my hand. Look.'

Ned held out his warty hand for his brother's inspection, and the chicken, seizing its chance, flew out of Jem's arms and, pausing only to give him a farewell peck on the cheek, ran into the far corner of the yard, cackling angrily.

'Oh, Lor', why'd you let it go, you stupe?' cried Ned. 'If that chicken isn't plucked by the time Ma gets back she'll give us a wallopin'.'

'Well, I'm not goin' after it,' retorted Jem, rubbing his bloodied cheek. 'Here, I tell you what, though, we could do somethin' that'd make her real happy. There's a load of rats in the sty that keep eatin' all the grub Ma puts out for the pig. Why don't we catch them, eh? I'll get up on the roof and shout and bang about a bit to frighten them and then they'll come rushin' out and . . .'

'And I'll catch them and wring their necks,' said Billy, jumping up and down in excitement.

'Don't be soft,' growled Jem, pushing his little brother aside, 'you'd never get nowhere near them. Ned'll clobber them with his catapult.'

'So what'll I do?' demanded Billy, in the high, petulant voice of an angry five-year-old.

'You open the door of the sty when I tell you.'

Billy pouted. 'I never get to do none of the important stuff.'

'Openin' the door *is* the most important stuff,' said Jem, winking at Ned. 'You got to open it just right – wide enough to let the rats out but not so wide as you let the pig out as well, see?'

'Get on with it then,' said Ned, loading his catapult with a small pebble. 'Ma'll be home any minute.'

'Right oh, here we go.' And clambering on to the roof of the sty Jem began to jump about and shout so loudly that every rat in London bolted for cover.

Now the plan would have worked beautifully if it hadn't been for Billy. As he ran to the door he slipped on a piece of wet cabbage, grabbed at the bolt and fell back on his bottom. The door flew open and the pig, terrified by the din Jem was making on the roof, ran out of the sty, followed by a large rat.

'Nab it!' Jem yelled, jumping down. 'Not the rat, Ned, the pig. If that pig gets away, Ma'll skin us alive. And do somethin' useful, Lor's sake, Billy. Don't just stand there rubbin' your bum.'

'But it hurts,' he whined.

'It'll hurt a sight more if Ma comes back and finds that pig gone,' cried Jem, hurling himself at the pig and hanging on to its neck.

There was a great deal of shouting and squealing as the boys and the pig chased round and round the yard, splashing through smelly puddles, wading through piles of garbage and manure and tripping over an assortment of flea-bitten dogs and mangy cats.

At the height of the uproar a young man

swaggered into the yard and looked about him with a bemused expression on his face. 'Well, well, so this is Devil's Acre. I can see it ain't the fashionable part of town,' he drawled, putting a monocle to his eye. 'And I can smell it ain't, neither,' he added, taking a perfumed handkerchief from his pocket and holding it to his nose. 'It's weally wather dweadful.'

The three boys stopped dead and the pig, who was tired after all the running around, began to root contentedly among the rotting vegetables.

'*Weally wather dweadful?*' Jem mimicked him, pretending to put a monocle to his eye. 'I say, Ned, it's *weally wather dweadful* here, ain't it?' And pulling a grimy scarf from his neck he blew his nose on it.

'You mucky little bwat, don't you know it's fashionable for a gen'leman to lisp?' snapped the young man. 'Not that you'd know anythin' about gen'lemen or fashion. Where did you get that disgustin' wideawake?'

'What's wrong with it?' said Jem indignantly, for his exceedingly dirty, greasy hat with its low crown and wide brim was one of his proudest possessions.

'It's about six sizes too big, that's what.'

Jem, the oldest of the three brothers, was a short, stocky boy with a pug nose and eyes as black and bright as a terrier's. He rather fancied himself a man about town in his long coat, waistcoat and spats. The fact that his waistcoat was held together with string, his coat hung in tatters and one of his trouser legs was missing seemed not to bother him at all.

'You a dipper, guv?' he asked.

'Just cos I'm well dwessed it don't signify I'm a pickpocket,' the man sniffed. And he pushed back his cutaway jacket to reveal a richly brocaded waistcoat with the chain of a gold fob watch dangling from one pocket and a scarlet cravat held in place by a large diamond pin.

Jem devoured the diamond with his eyes and it was all he could do to stop himself from reaching out to snatch it. Such a jewel would have kept him and his brothers in food and drink for many a year, but any child caught stealing was given a flogging with the birch or sent to prison.

'To tell the twuth,' the man bent down and beckoned the boys towards him with his ebony cane, 'I'm the son of a duke. But don't tell nobody cos my pa don't like me associatin' with common people the likes of you.'

'Nah, well, *our* pa don't like us associatin' with half-baked people the likes of you,' said Jem, offended by the stranger's arrogance, 'so why don't you shove off?'

'As a matter of fact I got legitimate business in these parts,' snapped the man. 'I'm lookin' for a fortune-teller.'

'What for?'

'To tell my fortune, of course, you ninny.'

'What's a fortune?' asked Billy.

'It's what's goin' to happen in the future. My dog's fightin' another dog in a important match and I want to know if it's goin' to win.'

'Why?'

'Look, I'm not standin' here answerin' daft questions all day,' said the man irritably. 'Does a Madam Natasha live here or not? She's a . . .' he pulled a scrap of paper from his pocket and read out, 'palmist, herbalist and cwystal ball weader. Lucky charms and magic potions extwa.'

'That's our gran,' said Ned.

'Your gwan's Madam Natasha?' The man stared at him in disbelief.

'Nah, that's just a silly name she calls herself. Her real name's Doris Perkinski.'

'What?' The stranger gave Ned a patronizing smile. 'You mean Perkins, don't you?'

'Nah, I don't. It's Perkinski.'

'Perkinski?' The man threw back his head and roared with laughter.

'What's so funny about that?' demanded Jem hotly.

'It's . . . it's widiculous,' the man gasped, tears running down his cheeks. 'Nobody's called Perkin*ski*.'

'Well we are. What's your name then?'

'Tom Wamsbottom . . . I mean, *The Hon* Tom Wamsbottom.'

'What's a hon?' said Billy.

'It's a gen'leman what comes fwom an awistocwatic family, like what I do. Now where's this Dowis Perkin*ski*?'

'Gran lives there,' said Ned, pointing to a ramshackle old caravan resting on its shafts in the corner of the yard, its big wooden wheels broken and bits of straw sticking out of the chimney on its roof.

'She doesn't live with us in our caravan no more,' said Billy, pointing to a slightly smarter one in the other corner, 'cos Pa says she makes horrible smells.'

'It's her magic potions,' explained Ned quickly.

'Is she a witch then?' the young man asked suspiciously.

'Nah, she's a gypsy. We're all gypsies.'

'You? Gypsies?' Tom Ramsbottom sniggered. 'You don't look much like gypsies to me. I thought they had olive skins and black hair and they played the fiddle and danced a lot.'

'Oh, we do, we do,' protested Jem, pulling Billy's cap well down over his ears to hide his dirty blond curls. 'We practically fiddled our fingers off. And you should see my sister, Kate, she's worn her legs down to stumps with dancin' and stuff.'

'And if you don't believe us we'll get Pa to flatten you,' said Billy, smiling sweetly. 'Our pa's a prize frighter.'

'A prize fighter,' Ned corrected him.

'Oh yeh?' sneered Tom.

'It's true. He's called Bert the Beast and he's the best fighter in Westminster.'

'Pa's the best in the whole of London,' Jem said. 'And he gets real nasty when people don't believe we're gypsies,' he added darkly.

The man gulped and stepped back. 'All right, all right, I believe you. Now go and tell Madam Na . . . I mean, your gwan that I'm here.'

'I will,' cried Billy. And clambering up the rickety steps to his grandmother's caravan he hammered on the door, 'Gran, Gran, open up, plaguy quick!'

After a minute or two the door opened a crack and an old woman peered round it. 'What's all the shindy?' she demanded. 'Oh, it's you, Billy. You bang

on my door again, you little varmint, and I'll give you such a clout round the ear'ole . . .'

'But, Gran, there's a mug wants to see you,' cried Billy.

'A what? Oh . . .' Gran's eyes lit up when she saw the dashing young man waiting in the court-yard.

'He's the son of a duke,' Billy whispered in her ear.

'Lawks a mercy! Please come in, Your Dukeness,' she gushed, opening her door with a flourish. 'And you lot, hook it!' she barked at her grandsons, knocking Billy off the step with a well-aimed back of the hand.

'So what'll we do now?' said Jem.

'Let's go and do wheels in the Square,' suggested Billy, who loved the excitement of turning cart-wheels among the horse-drawn cabs, carriages and buses in Trafalgar Square.

'Nah,' said Jem, 'we don't get enough money for it. Leastways, not enough to justify gettin' ourselves run over for.'

'We could clean boots,' suggested Ned.

'*Clean boots?*' Jem recoiled in horror. 'That's work, that is. 'Sides, we'd need a box and brushes.'

'What about sellin' birds' nests then? That bloke in the Haymarket says he gets twopence for a blackbird's nest.'

'Oh, that's a crack idea, Ned,' said Jem archly. 'Billy, just climb up that tree and get a couple of blackbirds' nests, will you?'

Billy looked at the dilapidated tenement houses, crumbling walls and broken fences that surrounded Devil's Acre. There was not a tree, bush, branch, twig or leaf in sight. 'What tree?' he said, puzzled.

'All right, don't get snaggy,' muttered Ned as Jem scowled at him. 'It was just an idea.'

'Yeh, well if somebody doesn't come up with a better one before Ma gets back we'll . . . Hey up, look sharp! Here she comes.'

The three boys dodged behind a water butt and cowered down as a woman plodded wearily into the yard. She was dressed in a strange array of old clothes: a long, bedraggled skirt, lace-up boots with more cracks and holes than leather, a faded shawl drawn around her thin shoulders and a battered, brimless straw boater on her greying hair.

'All right, you can come out of there, you lot,' she shouted, lifting from her neck a big tray filled with ornaments, combs, paper flowers, pieces of lace and a dozen or so other knick-knacks of no great use to anyone.

'Ullo, Ma,' said Jem sheepishly as the three brothers emerged from their hiding place.

'Don't you "Ullo, Ma" me!' she scolded him. 'What's that pig doin' out? We're supposed to be fattenin' it up for Christmas, not runnin' its legs off.'

'Well . . . er . . . you see, Ma, there was a huge hurricane that took the roof of its sty clean off and it jumped over the side and . . .'

'Don't go givin' me none of your sappy stories, Jem, or I'll give you the back of my hand. Get that pig back in. Now!'

'Why're we fattenin' it, Ma? We never get to eat it,' said Billy.

'But we get a lot of money when we sell it, son. Like the chicken Gran killed this mornin'. It was a real fat'un, so we should get a tidy sum for it.'

'But Gran didn't kill that chi—'

'Did you have any luck today, Ma?' Jem cut in quickly before Billy could put his mother in an even worse temper.

'Not bad.' She put a hand in the pocket of her

ragged skirt and pulled out some coins. 'This is doin' me a power of good,' she said, pointing to a large sign hanging from her tray.

'Who wrote it for you, Ma?'

'Old man Stephens. And he only charged me a penny. Nice, eh?'

'What's it say?'

'It says somethin' like, "I'm a poor widow woman with twenty kids to support,"' said his mother, reciting it by heart because neither she nor her boys could read. '"I'm deaf, dumb and blind and my babies are starvin'. For mercy's sake spare a penny or two."'

'But you're not deaf, dumb and blind, are you, Ma?' asked Billy.

'Of course I'm not, you ninny, but other people don't know that, do they? Now go on, up the Strand, the lot of you. Your pa'll warm your backsides if he finds you here doin' nothin'. And Ned, you take the shallow, son,' said his mother, pointing to her tray.

'Oh, Ma, it's so heavy it nearly rips my head off,' whined Ned.

'You do what I tell you or the Terror'll get you,' she snapped. 'Then you'll be sorry.'

'You're always on about the Terror, Ma,' Ned said

as he picked up the tray and put the strap around his neck. 'Who is he?'

'If I was to tell you about him it'd give you nightmares, son,' she said darkly. 'Just be thankful you never met him — and I hope you never will.'

2

To get to the Strand, one of London's most fashionable streets, the three boys had to walk through alleys so narrow that a person leaning out of one window could shake hands with someone leaning out of the window opposite.

In these dark, dingy passageways lived men, women and children, thousands of them, packed together in small houses with damp, rotting floors and crumbling walls, their broken windows stuffed with brown paper, their doors torn off for firewood. With no lights, except smoky candles, no bathroom, no lavatory and no heating, these Londoners lived hard lives in horrible surroundings, making a living any way they could. Many were honest. Many more were driven to crime.

'Watch your tray, Ned,' cautioned Jem, staying close to his brother. 'That lot'll get nicked if you're not careful.'

The throng of people in the Strand was just as

dense as that in the neighbouring slum streets, but here there were elegant gentlemen in frock coats and extraordinarily high top hats that made their owners look very tall and impressive. Alongside them walked their wives and daughters in long dresses with full, flounced skirts over three or four petticoats, cashmere shawls or cloaks, ruched silk bonnets, dainty boots in softest leather and kid gloves or silk mittens.

Here too were shops filled with goods, some with the royal coat of arms over the door, their owners running out to greet the smart carriages as they drew up.

Horse-drawn hansom cabs and elegant broughams and chaises carried the rich up and down the streets while barefoot urchins dressed in rags dodged in and out between the wheels, risking their lives among the flying hoofs to sweep the street crossings clean of mud and horse manure.

'Look out, Ned, here comes a likely gull.' Jem nudged his brother as a woman, dressed warmly against the autumn chill in a velvet cape and fur muff, got out of a smart little carriage and pair.

'Nah,' Ned hung back. 'Not her.'

'Why not?'

'Cos she looks a nice old codger.'

'You off your chump or somethin'?' snapped Jem.

'That's just the sort we want.' And turning to Billy he gave him a resounding whack around the ears.

Billy let out a loud wail and burst into tears, at which Jem put his arm around him protectively.

'Why, whatever's the matter with the little fellow?' exclaimed the woman anxiously. 'Is he in pain?'

'Please, missus, he's upset cos he can't stop himself thinkin' about our poor dear father who was drowned,' said Jem, pinching Billy's bottom hard so that he cried all the louder.

'Drowned?' she repeated in horror.

'Yeh, he was the captain of a big boat and one day it hit an island and sank to the bottom of the sea. About a hundred . . . Nah, more like a thousand miles down it went, too far to get Pa back up again leastways, so now we're all alone in the world, missus, me and my little brothers.'

'Here, leave off,' grumbled Ned. 'I'm not little.'

Ned was a year younger than Jem, but already an inch or so taller, which was a source of pride for Ned, but torment for his brother.

'But don't you have a mother?' asked the woman, whose eyes were beginning to glisten with tears.

'Course we do,' said Billy, who had stopped crying to listen to Jem's story. 'Our ma's back at—'

'My little brother was just goin' to say that our

ma's *back* broke when she was workin' down the mines,' explained Jem, giving Billy such a dig in the ribs that he burst into loud sobs again. 'She had to carry tons of coal and it done her in.'

'Oh, my goodness!' cried the woman, deeply distressed. 'What can I do to help you poor things?'

'If you could find it in your heart to give us some money, missus, just so's we could buy a few crusts . . .' suggested Jem.

'Or a pork pie,' said Billy.

'Perhaps I could buy something from you,' said the woman, picking up a piece of lace from Ned's tray. 'How pretty. Is it from Brussels?'

Jem nodded eagerly, wondering where Brussels was and what it had to do with lace anyway.

'Nah, it isn't,' piped up Billy. 'Ma made it.'

'Before she died,' added Jem quickly.

'But I thought you said she worked in the coal mines,' said the woman.

'She did, she did,' agreed Jem. 'But she sat up all night makin' lace as well.'

'Oh, so it isn't from Brussels then?'

'Yeh, it is. Ma was in Brussels at the time.'

The woman looked puzzled.

'And Kate makes paper flowers,' Billy beamed up at her. 'She's my big sister.'

'He means she used to make them before she died,' cut in Jem, treading on Billy's bare toes to shut him up.

'Your sister's dead too?' exclaimed the woman, aghast at so many tragedies in one family.

'Course not. She sings in the bar at the Dog 'n Bacon,' said Billy.

'And now she's singin' in heaven,' Jem corrected him. 'You'll have to forgive my brother, missus, he's a bit queer in the attic. It's cos he had the plague when he was a baby and it rotted his brain clean away.'

'Poor child.' The woman looked at Billy sadly. 'Here,' she reached into a pocket in her skirt and drew out a purse from which she took a penny, 'take this.'

Jem snatched the coin, bit it to make sure it was the real thing and put it in a pouch tied round his waist, where it was safe from pickpockets.

'Hey!' protested Billy. 'She was givin' it to me. I was goin' to buy a pork pie and . . .'

'Don't be soft, Billy,' said Ned. 'You know we got to take everythin' home to Ma.'

'Hold your jaw, Ned!' growled Jem under his breath.

But the woman had heard the remark.

'I thought you said you didn't have a mother,' she said, beginning to look at them with suspicion.

'Yeh . . . I mean . . . Oh!' Jem let out a cry of dismay, 'Oh Lor', we got to go. Sorry, missus.' And grabbing Ned and Billy he rushed them down the street at the double.

'What you doin'?' shouted Ned, trying to prize himself free of his brother's vice-like grip. 'Let go! I'll drop this pesky tray in a minute.'

'Crusher!' hissed Jem, looking nervously over his shoulder at the policeman who had suddenly appeared in the distance. 'Saw him comin' right at us, I did. It was old Bandy Shanks. And he recognized us too.'

'And I wager that old woman'll tell him what we did,' panted Ned as they ran across Trafalgar Square. 'And one day he'll catch us at it.'

'Nah, he'll never catch us. We're too leary . . . Billy, what you do that for?' Jem snapped as the little boy pinched his arm. 'You do that again and I'll . . .'

'I want my penny.'

'Jem, don't give it him,' admonished Ned.

'But I'm hungry, I want some of *them*.' Billy pointed to a man selling hot eels from a donkey and cart parked at the kerb.

'We got to take the money home to Ma,' insisted Ned.

'Not all of it,' said Jem slyly.

'Jem, if Ma ever finds out that you're cheatin' her . . .'

'Nah, she won't, she's no idea . . . And them eels do look uncommon tasty,' said Jem, whose mouth was beginning to water.

'Come on then,' said Billy, pulling him along. 'Come on.'

'Well, maybe just a small one . . . Hey up!' Jem stopped dead, staring at a young man swaggering along the road towards them, swinging his cane and raising his top hat to all the ladies, 'Isn't that bloke old Ramsbottom?'

'Which one?'

'The one with the sideburns like Eppin' Forest.'

'Oh yeh, so it is.'

'Wonder if Gran lifted his gold watch?' said Jem thoughtfully. 'Let's go and see.' And running up to the man he raised his wideawake in a mocking salute and said, 'Good afternoon, Your Royal Highness.'

The man looked startled for a moment and backed away.

'He's still got it,' Jem muttered in Ned's ear, 'and

the sparks.' He nodded at the diamond in the man's cravat. 'Gran must be losin' her touch.'

'Oh, it's you,' said the man, recognizing him. And raising his hat in an equally mocking salute he drawled, 'Good afternoon, Your Common Lowness. Still pwetendin' to be a gypsy, are you? Perkins*ki* . . . Huh!' he scoffed.

'I told you before,' growled Jem, 'we're not pretends.'

'What a load of hornswoggle,' sneered the man. 'You're just beggars puttin' on airs.'

'And you're just a block'ead puttin' on airs. Son of a duke . . . Huh! More like the son of a dummy, you ask me.'

Tom scowled and was about to say something equally scathing when Billy cried impatiently, 'Jem, I want some hot eels,' and began tugging his brother's coat-tails.

Tom looked at the little boy intently, running his eye over him in a calculating way as if he were sizing up a horse he was planning to buy, and said, 'Hungwy, are you, young'un?'

'Starvin'.' Billy nodded.

'Hmm . . .' Tom continued to look at the boy thoughtfully, then he reached into his pocket, took

out a threepenny bit and tossed it to Jem. 'Go and get some hot eels for all of us,' he said.

Jem caught the coin and stared at the man, open-mouthed.

'Cos I'm suddenly feelin' genewous, see,' Tom laughed. 'But you'd best not dawdle else I might change my mind.'

'Quick!' cried Billy, beginning to run.

'Not you, young'un,' said Tom, grabbing Billy and pulling him back. 'You stay here with me.'

'Why? Why?'

'Cos I don't want your bwothers wunnin' off with my money, that's why.'

There was a woman ahead of Jem and Ned buying eels, and the two boys waited with growing impatience while she made up her mind whether she wanted them hot or cold, with juice or without.

Jem glanced over his shoulder. Tom Ramsbottom was bending over Billy, talking to him earnestly, but the little boy was struggling to get away, spitting at him and kicking his shins.

'Look at that little varmint,' Jem said, nudging Ned.

'He's worried we'll eat the eels before he gets any, the greedy guts,' laughed Ned.

'Well, hurry up, you two,' interrupted the man selling eels. 'D'you want anythin' or not?'

'How much are they, guv?' Jem asked.

'Six pieces for a ha'penny.'

'Right, we'll have four cups, hot. And put in loads of juice too.'

'There you are then,' said the man, reaching into a large tin pot. 'Them's the best eels in London, all young'uns, fresh caught this mornin'. You can still hear them cryin' for their mothers.'

'They nice and spicy, guv?'

'Spicy? You'd think I'd poured a pint of gin in them, son.'

'I'm just goin' to try one,' said Jem, popping a particularly succulent morsel into his mouth. 'Cor, that was golopshus,' he sighed, closing his eyes in ecstasy as the baby eel slid down his throat.

'And they only cost twopence,' said Ned, helping himself to one. 'So there's a penny over.'

'Yeh, but don't tell old Ramsbottom. We'll pocket the penny and . . . Hey, where is he? Where's he gone?'

'And where's Billy?' said Ned, looking around in alarm.

'There they are!' Jem pointed.

Tom Ramsbottom was hurrying along the street,

carrying Billy, his hand clamped firmly over the little boy's mouth. Every now and then he lashed at him with his cane to stop him struggling, but Billy still pummelled and kicked him, his eyes wide with fear.

'Oy!' shouted Ned. 'You . . .!'

'Hold your jaw,' warned Jem. 'Go after him, Ned, he's headin' for the Haymarket, but don't let him see you. I'll go round the other way.'

'Here, is there somethin' wrong with my eels?' exclaimed the eel seller indignantly as the boys threw the cups in the gutter. But they were away, Ned dodging in and out of doorways and hiding behind people as he followed Tom Ramsbottom, and Jem flying up Whitcomb Street and along Orange, his mind racing with thoughts of kidnap and murder, for hundreds of children went missing from the streets of London every year.

As he turned the corner into the Haymarket Jem came face to face with Tom, who had slowed his pace, thinking he was safe from pursuit. But at the sight of Jem he tucked Billy under one arm, pulled his cane from under the other and glared at Jem, defying him to come any closer.

'Get him, Ned!' yelled Jem to his brother, and the man turned, startled. Seizing the opportunity, Jem

charged at him and began striking him on the chest and kicking his shins while Ned bashed him with his tray and Billy, who had tumbled to the ground, grabbed him round the knees and hung on.

The man flailed at the two older boys with his cane and, freeing himself from Billy, who was trying to bite a chunk out of his thigh, he ran off, cursing loudly.

'Cor, that was a close shave,' said Ned, putting a comforting arm around Billy's shoulders, 'he nearly nabbed you, he did.'

'Pick up your stuff plaguy quick, Ned, or it'll get pinched,' said Jem, who was concerned with rescuing the bits and bobs that had fallen from Ned's tray. 'You too, Billy. Don't stand there grizzlin'.' And the three boys scrabbled around the pavement anxiously.

'Oh drat!' groaned Ned.

'What's up?'

'Them garters Ma got in Petticoat Lane — they've gone. And the mirror and . . . Oh, Lor', the tinder-box's been nicked too. Ma'll kill me.'

'It's all right, child,' said a well-dressed young woman, bending over him. 'I rescued them for you.' And she put the missing items in his tray.

'Cor, thanks, missus,' he said with heartfelt gratitude. 'You saved my bacon, you have.'

'What was that wretched man doing?' she asked.

'Tryin' to grab my brother.'

'Oh, how dreadful. You poor little thing,' she said, turning to Billy. And reaching into her purse she gave him a penny.

Billy jumped up and down excitedly. 'Let's get some hot eels,' he cried, the horror of his attempted abduction quickly forgotten at the prospect of food.

'Nah, we got to take it back to Ma,' said Jem, prizing the penny out of Billy's hand.

'But . . .'

'If we go home empty-handed we'll be in for it, you know that,' said Jem. 'Anyway, you eat too much of them eels, they'll give you the collywobbles.'

'But I haven't eaten *any*,' Billy whined.

'Good. Then you won't get the collywobbles, will you?'

A sly look appeared in Billy's eye. 'If you don't buy me some, I'll tell Ma that man tried to nab me and it was your fault.'

'What d'you mean our fault?' Jem demanded hotly.

'Cos you shouldn't have left me with him. Ma's always tellin' you to keep an eye on me,' said the little boy with a smug smile because he knew he'd got the upper hand for once.

'He's right,' Ned nodded. 'Ma'd tan the skin off our hides if she found out.'

'Oh, all right,' Jem conceded. 'But just one cup, Billy, just one – and you got to share it with Ned and me.'

The journey back to Devil's Acre was slow. The boys dawdled, stopping every now and then to enjoy the Punch and Judy shows, the acrobats and jugglers, the stilt-walkers and dancing bears, the fiddlers and singers of ballads. On every street corner someone was selling their talent, or lack of it, for a halfpenny or farthing to buy food and shelter against the coming night.

By the time they got back to their caravan it was dark and their mother was angry.

'Your pa will be back in a minute and I don't want you gettin' under his feet,' she grumbled. 'Now eat your supper and go to bed quick as you can.' And she put a small piece of bread and a bowl of hot water with a potato and some cabbage in it in front of each of them.

It was the same meal every night, except on Sundays, when she made a potato pie and took it to the baker to be cooked in his oven, or if one of the family had been lucky enough to 'find' a stray chicken in a neighbouring yard they had a little meat.

The boys drank their soup, wiped their cracked and grimy bowls with the bread and washed down their dismal meal with foul-tasting water that had stood for days in a half-rotted barrel in the yard, its surface covered with dust and dirt.

'Did you get anythin' today?' asked their mother, keeping one ear cocked for her husband's footsteps.

'Only tuppence, Ma,' said Jem, winking slyly at Ned for he still had a penny left. And he lifted his waistcoat and took two of the three coins out of the pouch around his waist and handed them to her.

'It's not much,' said Ma, biting on the coins before stuffing them down the front of her bodice. 'You'll have to do a lot better tomorrow.'

All was not well with Gran either.

'What's up with her?' said Jem as a loud wailing came from the direction of the old woman's caravan. 'She feelin' all overish again?'

'Nah, she's well enough, son, but it's that bloke that came to see her this afternoon,' said his mother. 'He pinched the pearl brooch your grandpa stole for her when they were courtin'.'

'You don't mean The Hon Ramsbum?' cried Billy

fearfully, remembering the man who had tried to kidnap him.

'The Hon indeed!' sniffed his mother. 'No gen'le-man would've done somethin' wicked as that to a poor, unsuspectin' old woman. But I reckon he must be the sharpest thief in London to gull your gran,' she added, half admiringly.

'Nah, he's not the sharpest, Ma,' said Jem.

'What d'you mean?' She frowned.

'I mean old Ramsbottom'll probably be missin' these about now,' he smirked. And he drew from his pocket the young man's gold watch and diamond pin.

3

It was Gran's seventieth birthday and her family and friends had filled Devil's Acre to overflowing to celebrate her prodigious age.

All the Perkinskis paraded in what they imagined gypsies wore at such times — the men in velveteen coats and corduroy caps, the women in brightly coloured skirts and tight bodices. Many of the younger girls were swathed in a profusion of large silk handkerchiefs from neck to ankle, with rings on their fingers and in their ears and heavy bangles jangling on their wrists. But it was Gran Perkinski who stole the show in a long, red frilly dress she had bought for twopence from a stall in Petticoat Lane market — which almost fitted her with the aid of several dozen pins — and black satin shoes with holes cut out to ease her bunions.

The shabby courtyard resounded to raucous shouts and laughter but Cousin Emma, normally a jolly woman with a ready wit, sat in a corner looking glum.

'What's up, my tulip?' asked Gran.

'It's my Ernie. He's doin' time.'

'What? Ernie in prison again?'

'Five years' hard labour,' wailed Cousin Emma, dabbing at her cheek with the edge of her apron. 'Five years on the treadmill just for forgin' a few coins.'

'It's a cryin' shame, Em,' said Pa Perkinski, easing himself into the chair next to her and putting a comforting arm around her shoulders. 'Lot of kerfuffle about nothin', if you ask me. But then there's no justice in this world, is there?' he said sadly. 'Leastways, not for the likes of us.'

'You look as if you've come to a bit of grief yourself, Bert,' she said. 'Someone's made a right mess of your mug.'

Pa was indeed a sorry sight with his battered nose and two black eyes. He had gone forty-five rounds with the Bermondsey Basher at the big fight in Spitalfields Market the previous night and definitely come off the worse.

But Pa had other, more important, reasons for being down in the mouth. He had visited the pawnshop that morning with the gold fob watch and diamond pin Jem had stolen from Tom Ramsbottom, his head full of plans for spending the small fortune that such expensive jewellery would surely bring. But his hopes had been cruelly dashed by the pawnshop owner, who informed him tartly that the watch was made of solid tin and the diamond was just a bit of glass. He offered Pa sixpence for the lot, take it or leave it. Grumbling about how nobody could be trusted any more, not even thieves, Pa took it.

'Give us a tune on your fiddle, Nick,' he said mournfully to one of his brothers. 'I could do with a bit of cheerin' up, straight I could.'

It was the moment everybody had been waiting for. Next to eating and drinking there was nothing the Perkinskis enjoyed more than dancing. As Uncle Nick picked up his violin and started to play they all leaped to their feet and threw themselves about with wild abandon.

Uncle Percy, who made a handsome living collecting dog dung from the streets and selling it at eight pence a bucket to the leather tanners, leaped on a table and did his own version of the Sailor's Hornpipe, which involved a good deal of jumping up and a good deal more of falling down, since he had imbibed rather too well of Pa's home-made potato wine.

Gran Perkinski did a wild gypsy dance with Cousin Jim, who worked for a butcher and had helped himself to a generous selection of pig's trotters, ox tongues, pigeon pies and cow's heels for the party. Normally a sober man who lived quietly with his wife and eighteen children over a pub in Lambeth, Cousin Jim and Gran leaped and twirled with such noisy enthusiasm that Old Mother Perry, a cantankerous neighbour, leaned out of her window and emptied the contents of her chamber pot over their heads.

At three in the morning, Kate, the Perkinskis' daughter, came back from the pub where she worked long hours as a barmaid. A red-haired girl of fourteen, with so many freckles on her face she looked as if she'd been sunbathing under a sieve, Kate's ambition was to be a singer, and when she wasn't serving tankards of ale and porter to the customers of the Dog and Bacon she tormented them with mawkish songs about jilted lovers and fatherless children.

Her arrival at Devil's Acre was greeted with cries of, 'Give us a song, Kate!' by those who were too drunk to remember what an ear-shattering experience it was, and before the sober ones could stop her she launched into 'The Widow's Last Prayer' in a tuneless shriek.

Jem put his hands over his ears, rolled his eyes

and began to howl like a dog sitting on a cactus. Ned and Billy followed suit. The louder Kate sang the louder they howled until finally she lost her temper.

'Pa!' she cried, stamping her foot. 'Them pesky brats should be in bed.'

'Yeh, you're right,' he agreed. 'Go on, you lot, and quick about it.'

'But Pa . . .'

'You heard what I said.'

'Kate always spoils everythin',' grumbled Jem as the three boys settled down on the straw mattress they shared in their parents' caravan. 'I don't see the point of sisters, straight I don't. If you ask me they should all be put in a pot and boiled.'

Just before dawn the guests began to tire and one by one, yawning and groaning, they sloped off into the early morning mist, muttering sleepy farewells. Jem, Ned and Billy slept soundly for an hour or so until their mother shook them awake.

'Get up and quick about it,' she said. 'There's work to be done, especially as your pa's not up to it, and don't come back empty-handed, you hear, or you'll get no supper.'

'But what about breakfast, Ma?' said Billy, yawning.

'Breakfast? You had enough to eat last night to last you a month. Now get goin'.'

'I'm not carryin' that tray again,' said Ned, whose head felt three times larger than normal. 'It's too heavy.'

'And I'm not doin' carterwheels neither,' said Billy.

'Oh, stop moanin' . . . Hey up, I know what,' cried Jem. 'We'll do the Scaldrum Dodge. That always goes immense.'

'Nah, I don't think we should do that again,' said Ned doubtfully.

'What's wrong with it?'

'We'll get done for cheatin', that's what.'

'How d'you make that out?' Jem protested. 'We're just dressin' up and havin' a bit of fun. If people're sappy enough to give us money that's not our fault, is it? Come on, we'll get Gran to help us.'

But Gran was in no condition to help anyone. She had celebrated her birthday more well than wisely and when the boys hammered on the door of her caravan she growled at them to clear off.

'She's probably feelin' a bit peaky this mornin',' whispered Ned, backing away, for his grandmother could be very peevish when she was unwell. 'I reckon we should leave her alone.'

But Jem ignored him.

'Gran,' he shouted, 'you got to help us do the Scaldrum Dodge.'

Silence.

'Gran!'

Silence.

'We'll give you a quarter of the money we get.'

The door flew open.

'Half.'

'Oh, Gran . . .'

'Half.'

'All right, all right,' Jem conceded.

'Come in, sit down and keep quiet,' said the old woman. 'Now, which one of you's goin' to have the bad head?'

'Him,' said Jem and Ned pointing at Billy.

'Why me? It's always me?' he protested.

'Cos you're the smallest and if you don't do what we say we'll bash you,' Jem explained in a brotherly way.

'It's lucky I kept a bit of steak for myself,' said Gran, cutting a sliver from a particularly juicy one and placing it on Billy's forehead. And taking a filthy bandage she wound it tightly round and round his head until only the smallest speck of blood could be seen oozing through. Then she took a handful of white flour and rubbed it into the boy's face and neck until he looked like a ghost. A smear of black boot polish rubbed under each eye completed the picture of a sickly child with a ghastly head wound.

'Can't I eat some of the beef, Gran?' pleaded Billy. 'I'm starvin'.'

'You're always starvin', you little guts.' Gran pushed him aside and turned her attention to Ned.

'Right,' she said, 'I'm goin' to give you a burn. Where d'you want it?'

'On his chest,' suggested Jem. 'It gives people a horrible shock when they see it. A woman fainted last time.'

'Righto, lift your shirt, Ned,' said Gran, and she covered his chest with a thick layer of fatty white soap over which she sprinkled some strong vinegar. After a few minutes what appeared to be large, yellow blisters began to form.

While Gran had been working on his brothers Jem had strapped his ankle to his thigh and pulled on a pair of Pa's baggy trousers with one leg cut off halfway down. They were wide enough for the boy to get his doubled-up leg into them so that his knee looked like a pathetic stump dangling below.

Gran squeezed some blood out of the rest of the

steak and smeared it over the 'stump'. Then she stood back to admire her handiwork.

'Jammy,' she cackled. 'You could fool anyone. In fact, I'd give you money myself . . . if I was sappy enough to give my money away.'

'We'd best steer clear of the Strand,' said Jem. 'I saw the Harris kids up there the other day workin' the Scaldrum Dodge. Only you could see they weren't for real cos one of them had a beetroot under his bandage. A beetroot, I ask you!' he scoffed. 'Amateurs. Spoil it for us professionals, they do.'

Ned wanted to go down to the Pool of London and watch the barges on the Thames, their sails billowing in the breeze, their decks piled high with bales of hay to feed the thousands of horses that pulled London's carriages, cabs and buses. Billy wanted to go to the Mall in the hope of seeing Queen Victoria and her husband, Prince Albert, as they drove to and from Buckingham Palace. But Jem wanted to go to the huge market in Covent Garden where the costermongers bought fruit and vegetables to sell later in the day from their barrows and donkey carts . . .

So they set off for Covent Garden.

They made slow progress. Heavy-eyed and yawning they shuffled into Whitehall and across Trafalgar

Square, Jem on crutches, Billy fretting that his bloodstained bandage kept slipping down so he couldn't see where he was going and Ned beginning to feel a bit tight and itchy around his chest as the soap dried.

'This one'll do,' muttered Jem as a motherly looking woman came into view, 'she looks real soft . . . Well, go on, do somethin'' he hissed at his brothers, hobbling painfully towards her on his crutches.

Billy put a hand to his head and started wailing and Ned rather reluctantly wrapped his arms around his chest and groaned.

'Please, missus,' said Jem, raising his hat as the woman drew level with them, 'spare a coin for three poor little orphans that's suffered terrible accidents.'

'My goodness me,' she cried, 'whatever has happened to you, you poor creatures?'

'I got run over by a bus,' explained Jem. 'It cut my foot off and then while I was layin' in the road it rolled back and cut my leg off at the knee. I got the bits at home and the doctor says he could sew them back on if I liked, but I haven't got the money . . . Billy!' he hissed, as the little boy howled, 'Stow it, will you, she can't hear me proper . . . Now my brother,' Jem continued, nodding at Ned, who was patiently waiting his turn, 'my brother fell in a vat of boilin' oil . . . Show the lady, Ned.'

Ned lifted his shirt to show the huge blisters all over his chest.

'He's got burns and blisters all over his body, missus,' said Jem, 'but he can't show you cos some of them are on his . . .' he hesitated coyly.

'His bum,' piped up Billy.

'Quite so, quite so,' murmured the woman, blushing. 'But if he fell in a vat of burning oil, why didn't his head get burned as well?' she frowned, peering at Ned's face, which was suspiciously free of blisters.

'Oh, that's because . . . er . . . because . . . he was dunked,' said Jem, 'by my wicked stepfather, a horrible bloke. He picked my poor little brother up by his hair and . . .'

'I am *not* little,' snarled Ned.

'. . . And put him in the boilin' oil,' continued Jem, ignoring the interruption. 'And my baby brother,' he pointed to Billy, who had given up yowling and was vigorously picking his nose, 'was in bed up in his room,' said Jem, who had heard that rich children had beds of their own, unlike he and his brothers who all crammed into the same one, 'when all of a sudden a thunderbolt the size of a horse,

nah . . . nah, the size of an elephant, fell through the roof. Gave him a nasty wallop, it did, right through to his brain.'

'Want me to show you, lady?' cried Billy eagerly. 'I got a big hole in my head. You can almost see my tonsils.'

'No, no!' The woman shielded her eyes as Billy began to unwind the bandage. 'Oh, you poor child, how you have suffered,' she said, stroking his cheek. 'What can I do to help . . .?' She stopped in mid-sentence and looked at her hand. Her beautiful blue leather glove had turned white. 'What on earth . . .?' She shook her head, puzzled. 'Why, it's . . . it's flour,' she cried, realizing she had been duped. 'You little scoundrels!'

'Come on! Plaguy quick before the crushers get here!' Jem urged his brothers as the woman shouted, 'Police! Police!' at the top of her lungs.

Children caught cheating the public with tricks like the Scaldrum Dodge were brought up before a magistrate and whipped or fined, but Jem moved remarkably fast on his crutches and he and his brothers were soon out of danger.

But luck was not on their side. No amount of pleading, moaning or weeping moved the hearts of the citizens of London that cold November morning.

Many winced when they saw the pathetic trio hobbling towards them, palms outstretched. Others averted their eyes. But the vast majority simply didn't notice them. Sick, hungry children in ragged clothes, their faces and bare feet grimy with mud, were just a part of street-life in Victorian London, like gas lamps, barrel organs and dancing bears.

Just when Jem was about to con a few pennies out of a kindly vicar, the boys were spotted by a policeman.

'Get your togs off!' cried Jem. And he unstrapped his leg while Ned unrolled the bandage from Billy's head, wrapped the sliver of beef in it and put it in his pocket.

'Come on,' he said and, grabbing Billy's hand, he turned and ran.

Clamping his helmet firmly on his head and swinging his rattle the policeman chased them up St Martin's Lane and into Long Acre. But the boys ran faster, dodging down backstreets, through darkened alleyways and courtyards until they were out of breath and could run no more.

'It's all . . . all right,' panted Jem. 'We lost him.'

'Yeh, and now we're lost too,' complained Ned. 'I don't recognize nothin' here. What we goin' to do?'

'Give me a minute to think,' said Jem, bending double. 'I got the stitch and . . . Billy! Billy, come back, you little varmint!'

But Billy wrenched himself free of Jem's hand, ran across the street and pressed his nose against the window of a grocer's shop, gazing in rapture at the huge hams, great rounds of cheese, crusty brown loaves, cakes, pastries and sweetmeats inside.

'Cor, look at all that,' he said as his brothers caught up with him. 'Isn't it splendiferous!'

'Yeh,' agreed Ned. 'But lookin' at food won't fill your belly.'

'But I'm starvin',' whimpered Billy, staring at a display of particularly succulent pork pies. 'Can't we get one of them?'

'What with?' retorted Ned. 'We haven't got the ready.'

'Nah, we got no money but we got brains, haven't we?' said Jem, winking. And he walked casually past the entrance and back again.

'Nobody in there,' he whispered, 'except the owner and his missus by the looks of it. Ned, got any soap left on you?'

His brother lifted his shirt, looked at his chest and nodded. Jem reached out to scrape some off, but Ned pushed his hand away. 'Nah, I'm not doin' it.'

 43

'Righto, I will,' said Jem.

'You'll get us all into trouble again.'

'Look, Ned,' Jem interrupted him angrily, 'you hungry or not?'

'Course I am.'

'So am I. And so's Billy. But we haven't made no money today, so we can't buy no grub, can we? And if we go home empty-handed we won't get no grub there neither. So, d'you want to eat or not?'

'Oh, all right,' Ned muttered. 'But this is the last time. Two of Cousin Maud's kids were caught doin' this dodge last week and now they're in clink.'

'But they were *caught*, weren't they?'

'Yeh, and we will be too.'

'Nah, we won't. We're too fly for that – leastways, I am,' boasted Jem. 'Now get on with it, you're wastin' time.'

Ned scraped a large sliver of soap from his skin and put it under his tongue. Throwing himself to the ground in the shop doorway, he thrashed from side to side, waving his arms and legs around like a windmill and uttering piteous cries.

'Help! Help! My brother's havin' a fit!' shouted Jem as the soapy foam gushed out of Ned's mouth. 'He's dyin'.'

Ned thrashed about twice as hard, rocking his

head from side to side, rolling his eyes, drumming his feet on the floor, gasping and shrieking when the shopkeeper and his wife came rushing out.

Billy was so impressed with his brother's performance he burst out laughing and clapped his hands until Jem cuffed him round the ear.

'Poor mite,' said the shopkeeper's wife, leaning over Ned, 'whatever can we do?'

'He gen'rally stops if he's held down,' said Jem. 'But you got to hold him real tight or he'll start up again and do himself a mischief. Last time he had a fit he bit his tongue clean off.'

'Well, it seems to have grown back,' said the shopkeeper, peering into Ned's mouth.

'Yeh, well . . . er . . . the doctor sewed it back on,' said Jem. 'Watch out, he's gettin' worse. Nab him or he'll kill himself.'

But Ned made quite sure neither the shopkeeper nor his wife could get hold of his arms and legs. Working himself into a frenzy he bounced up and down, while the foam poured in an endless stream over his chin and neck.

Meanwhile Jem ran into the shop and with many a guilty glance over his shoulder began thrusting pies, cheeses and crusty rolls down the front of his coat and into his pockets.

'Hey, what d'you think you're doing?' shouted a boy, appearing suddenly from the back of the shop.

Jem took one look at his startled face, ran out, grabbed Billy, shouted, 'Scarper!' to Ned, and made off down the street as fast as he could. Ned sprang up, knocking over his would-be helpers, spat out the rest of the soap and raced after his brothers.

Cries of, 'Stop, thief!' and, 'After them!' filled the air.

'Faster, Billy, faster!' Jem urged him on as the footsteps pounding behind them drew closer.

'I can't,' he gasped. 'I can't. My legs won't run no more.' And he stumbled and fell.

'In here, quick,' said Jem, pointing to a half-open gate leading to a dingy courtyard and, dragging Billy between them, he and Ned went in and crouched down. 'Don't say a word,' warned Jem, as the pounding footsteps grew louder. 'I'll tan your hide, Billy, if you make any noise.'

'Which way did they go?' shouted someone in the street.

'They went down there!'

'No, I saw them go that way!'

A crowd seemed to have joined in the chase, and the boys huddled together, scarcely daring to breathe, their eyes wide with fear.

'I'd know them if I saw them again,' cried a man whom Jem instantly recognized as the shopkeeper. 'One's a short, stocky lad with the wickedest pair of eyes I've ever seen in anybody's head and the other one's a beanpole with hair sticking up in clumps.'

'And they've got a little kid with them,' added his wife. 'Face like an angel – pity he hasn't got the soul to match.'

After a few minutes' confusion the crowd beyond the gate began to wander away. They had lost the scent and were beginning to lose interest as well.

'I think they must've gone,' whispered Jem. And he opened the gate and peered round it cautiously. 'Yeh, we've shaken them off. Come on, let's get goin'.'

'Let's eat first,' pleaded Billy.

'Yeh, what about all that grub?' said Ned. 'Come on, Jem, give it over.'

But Jem shook his head sadly. 'It all fell out when I was runnin'.'

'What, the whole lot?'

'Everythin'.'

'Crikey, all that work and all I got for it was a mouthful of soap. I knew I shouldn't have done it, I don't know why I listen to you,' complained Ned. And Billy burst into tears.

'Give him that bit of steak in your pocket, for Lor's sake,' said Jem. 'Anythin' to stop him snivellin'.'

It was a tired, dispirited little group that set out for Devil's Acre. And to add to their miseries the sulphurous smoke that belched from the thousands of chimneys across London had combined with the damp November air to make a heavy fog as thick and green as a plate of mushy peas. It swirled about the boys, stinging their eyes and filling their lungs until they choked and coughed.

'We're not goin' the right way,' said Ned, after they had trudged along in silence for several minutes.

'Course we are,' said Jem confidently, wondering where they were.

'I don't like this,' whimpered Billy, and he moved closer to Jem, clutching the tails of his brother's coat in his small fist.

As darkness fell the fog grew thicker, so thick the boys could barely see each other, though they were walking shoulder to shoulder.

'Stay close,' said Jem. 'Ned, take hold of my hand then we won't lose each other . . . Billy? Billy, where are you?'

'I'm here, Jem. I'm eatin' my bit of beef,' he said, chewing hungrily on the raw meat.

'Well, keep up.'

Disembodied voices floated on the foul air. Footsteps hurried past them.

'Shove on one side!' yelped Ned, as a drunken man lurched into them.

'Silly old codger,' muttered Jem, pushing him away.

A woman near by called, 'Effie! Effie!'

'Where are we, missus?' shouted Jem. 'We're lost.'

'You ain't lost, love,' came the reply. 'You're in St Giles in dear ol' London Town.'

'*St Giles?*' Jem gasped. All unwittingly he and his brothers had stumbled into the Rookery, the most dangerous slum in the city. Murderers, thieves and all manner of rogues lived here, London's poorest and most desperate people, all crammed together, chattering, squabbling, fighting, like a huge flock of hungry birds in a tree. Even Pa Perkinski, tough as he was, wouldn't go into the St Giles Rookery alone. And certainly not after dark.

'They'll slit your throat soon as look at you,' he'd told the boys grimly. 'You steer well clear of that place if you want to stay alive.'

Jem comforted himself with the thought that

the fog was providing a protective cover for him and his brothers and he kept his fingers crossed that it wouldn't lift till dawn. But where would they sleep that night and what would they do in the morning when everyone could see them, he wondered?

'I'm cold,' whined Billy. 'And I'm tired. And . . .'

'Shh!' warned Jem. 'Don't let no one hear us. If they don't know we're here, we won't come to no harm.'

There were voices all around them now, low mutterings and menacing whispers.

'I think we're bein' followed,' whispered Ned, constantly glancing over his shoulder. 'I can't see nobody but I know there's someone there.'

'Course there isn't,' Jem muttered, though he too could feel some presence dogging their footsteps. 'Cor blimey, what's that?' he shrieked as something brushed against his leg.

'It's just a cat.'

Startled, Billy dropped the piece of beef he'd been chewing and bent down, scrabbling about on the ground to find it. But his brothers, unaware that he had stopped, walked on.

'Wait! Wait for me!' Billy shouted, and started to run after them, but a pair of hands reached out from

the fog and grabbed him. He gave one scream of terror, and then a fist was thrust into his mouth, silencing him.

Hearing his brother's cry, Jem's heart gave a great lurch. 'Billy!' he cried, running back. 'Billy, where are you? Where are you?'

He turned and collided with Ned.

'What happened?'

'How do I know?'

'He must've fallen over.'

'But he screamed. Why did he scream?'

A thousand voices filled the night. But Billy's voice was not among them.

Jem and Ned ran back and forth and round and round in circles in the dense fog, calling, 'Billy! Billy!' at the tops of their voices, choking on the damp air.

'It's no good,' said Jem panting. 'He's . . . he's gone. I reckon he's been grabbed.'

'D'you think that man's got him, Jem? D'you think it was Ramsbottom? D'you think . . .?'

'I don't know. I don't know. I DON'T KNOW,' shouted Jem, his fear making him short-tempered. 'Anyone could've grabbed him.'

There was a long silence as Ned let the horror of this sink into his brain.

'What'll they do to him, Jem?' he whispered. 'Will they hurt him?'

'We got to get home. We got to tell Pa.'

'D'you think we'll ever see Billy again? D'you think . . .?'

'Hold your jaw,' growled Jem. And grabbing Ned's arm he set off in what he hoped was the direction of Devil's Acre.

4

Billy was so frightened he barely realized what was happening – the sudden flurry of footsteps, the steely hands that grabbed him, the muttered oaths as he struggled to escape. The sound of his brothers' voices calling his name grew fainter as he was hurried away through the swirling fog down dark, strange streets, deeper and deeper into the heart of the terrible Rookeries.

At last his kidnapper stopped before a door. Slinging Billy over his back as if he were a sack of coal he raised a fist and tapped a signal . . . *Tap ti ti tap tap.*

'Who is it?' came a sharp voice from inside.

'Me.'

'Who's me?'

'Mr Bullock, of course,' said the man gruffly. 'Who the devil d'you think it is?'

'Sorry, Mr B.'

The door opened and a boy stood in the doorway. Now Billy was used to dirt. His own skin was a dark shade of grey and his hair so matted no brush or comb could ever fight their way through it, but he had never seen anyone as grimy as the boy who stood to one side to let them in. His face, arms and legs were filthy, his clothes black and shiny with grease. Only his eyes shone white – and the three teeth he showed when he grinned, which he was doing at that moment.

'Hullo, Mr B,' he said. 'Been huntin', have you?'

'Yeh, I got a new nipper, Pete,' said the man, holding Billy up for inspection. 'Real jammy, ain't he? And just the right size for the job too.'

Billy struggled to free himself from the man's grip, squirming and kicking until he was red in the face.

'Well done, Mr B, looks as if you got a very promisin' item there,' said Pete. 'I see it's got a bit of fight in it too,' he added, as Billy tried to sink his teeth into the man's arm. 'Bring the little varmint closer to the light and let's take a look at him.'

Holding Billy at arm's length, Mr Bullock carried him into a small, cosy kitchen. A log fire crackled in the grate and an oil lamp flickered on a long trestle table in the middle of the room. A neat row of black boots stood by the door, and shirts, skirts, aprons and pantaloons in shades of grey hung from a rope

beneath the rafters stretched from one side of the room to the other.

A woman was standing at the coal-fired stove, stirring a saucepan, while a young girl set out dishes and cutlery on the table.

'Hello, my lovely,' said Mr Bullock, and the girl ran towards him with an ugly, hobbling gait.

Dumping Billy on the floor he picked her up and swung her round and round until she begged him to stop. 'You're makin' me giddy, Dad,' she laughed.

'Got a new climbin' boy, Clem,' he said, pointing at Billy, who was now cowering under the table. 'Get him out of there, Pete.'

Pete got down on his hands and knees and reached out to grab Billy, but the little boy scrambled to his feet and ran to the door, tugging at the handle.

'Stop him!' shouted Pete, and immediately two boys who had been hunched in a dark corner shot up and helped drag a screaming, struggling Billy back into the room.

'You little . . .!' growled the sweepmaster, lifting his arm.

'Nah, Dad, don't hit him,' pleaded the girl. 'He's only a baby.'

'Clem's right,' agreed Pete as the three boys circled round Billy, staring at him with critical eyes.

'You must've snatched him from his cradle, Mr B. How old are you, nipper?'

Billy held up one hand, stretching the fingers.

'Five? You don't look it.'

'What's your name?'

'Billy.'

'Billy what?'

'Billy Perkinski.'

'Perkin*ski*?'

'I'm a gypsy,' said Billy quickly before they all started to jeer.

'Don't be a stupe,' scoffed Mr Bullock. 'You're never no gypsy. I reckon someone's been pullin' your leg.'

'Don't matter, Billy, you're one of us now, you're a Matey. Come over here and warm your bones,' said Pete, pulling him towards the fire. 'This is Dick and Harry,' he nodded at the other two boys who were as caked with dirt as Pete was. 'The old party doin' the cookin's Mr B's missus,' he said, lowering his voice. 'Her bark's worse than her bite, so don't pay her much heed when she starts yellin' and screamin'. And Clem,' his face softened as he glanced over his shoulder at the girl, who was showing her father a sampler she had embroidered, 'she's all right. As for Mr B . . .' He shrugged. 'I reckon he's better than most sweepmasters. But don't never get on the wrong side of him.'

'What d'you mean?' whispered Billy, who'd never met a sweepmaster before.

'You'll find out,' muttered Pete.

'Supper ready yet, Flo?' said Mr Bullock, taking his place at the head of the table.

'It will be in a minute, my dear,' said his wife. 'But first I got to give this lot a bath.'

'What?' The boys backed away in horror.

'But we had one just two months ago, Mrs B,' protested Pete.

'Then you're about due another one. Him too,' she nodded at Billy. 'He looks as if he could do with it.'

'Nah, I don't,' said Billy in alarm. 'My ma says water's bad for you.'

'It'll be a lot worse for you if you don't do what Mrs Bullock says. Now get out there!' shouted the sweepmaster.

Muttering and grumbling under their breath the boys filed out into a small backyard and stood shivering in the freezing night air.

'Help me with them, Pete,' said Mrs Bullock, pointing to two buckets. 'And don't spill none. I had to queue for half an hour for that water and then the

standpipe broke, so we won't get no more for Lor' knows how long.'

'Right you are, Mrs B,' said the boy, pouring the cold water into a rusty old tub.

'So who's first?' she said.

'Him,' said the Mateys. And before Billy could escape they stripped off his clothes, all of them hand-me-downs from his brothers, from the big, floppy cap on his head to the ragged trousers rolled up to his knees.

Billy let out a shriek when he was plunged into the icy water and he shrieked even louder when Mrs Bullock set about him with a scrubbing brush and a large bar of carbolic soap that smelled of tar.

'You're scrapin' my skin off! I'll die. Stop it, missus!' he pleaded with her. But his cries fell on deaf ears.

'You could grow cabbages in your armpits,' she said, scouring them with the hard bristles. 'And I can tell that neck's never seen a drop of water. Now get your clothes back on,' she said, as he clambered out of the tub. 'And if you want to relieve yourself, the privy's over there.' She pointed to a hole in the ground over a cesspit. 'Right, Dick, it's your turn. Look sharp about it, lad.'

Protesting vigorously, Dick took off his filthy

clothes and stepped into the tub. But as Mrs Bullock began to scour and polish him the most amazing thing happened.

'Here,' said Billy, bending over the tub and touching the boy's skin in wonderment, 'you've turned pink.'

The three Mateys burst out laughing.

'That's what happens in our line of business, Billy,' said Pete. 'It's cos we're always covered in soot.'

'What's soot?'

'The stuff you find up your chimney.'

'I don't have no chimney.'

'Course you have. All houses have a chimney.'

'Ours hasn't.'

'Then it's not a proper house.'

Billy's face fell. 'It's got wheels,' he said, hoping that would make up for the lack of a chimney. 'And my pa gets Bessie to pull it when we move on.'

'Who's Bessie, your mum?'

'Nah, Bessie's our horse.'

'Oh, I get it, you live in a caravan.' Pete nodded. 'Well, you won't be needin' us then. We're chimney sweeps, you see. Leastways we used to be, only we've grown too big for it now, so we send littl'uns like you up the chimney to get the lie of the land,' he tapped the side of his nose and gave Billy a cunning smile, 'if you know what I mean.'

Billy didn't know what Pete meant. He'd never been up a chimney and couldn't imagine what land could be seen from inside one. 'What's the lie of the . . .?' he began. But Mrs Bullock cut him short.

'That's enough clackin' from you lot. And don't throw that away, you block'eads!' she exclaimed as Dick and Harry picked up the tub of water that was now so black and thick with soot it looked more like mud. 'Mr B'll have a wash in that later. Now come on, you.' She pushed Billy ahead of her into the kitchen. 'Sit there,' she pointed to a corner of the room furthest from the supper table, 'and keep quiet. I don't like a lot of noise when I'm eatin'. It upsets my digestion.'

'Cor,' Dick muttered as the woman put dishes full of steaming tripe and onions, baked potatoes and suet dumplings on the table, 'Look at all that, Pete.'

'I am lookin'. And lookin's all I'll do, cos we won't get none of it,' said the boy in a disgruntled voice.

'All we'll get is yesterday's scraps,' sighed Harry.

The scraps were a dish of cold potatoes, slimy cabbage, hard crusts and well-chewed bacon rinds that the sweepmaster's wife put on the floor for them.

'Eat up, nipper,' Pete urged Billy, ramming the fatty remains of a pork chop in his mouth and sucking the bone vigorously. But though his stomach was empty there was a lump as big as a fist in Billy's throat and he couldn't eat.

'Can I go home, Pete?' he whispered.

'Don't be daft, you got to stay here.'

'How long?'

'Long as Mr B wants you to.'

'Won't I never go home?'

'Well, I been here . . .' Pete counted on his greasy fingers, 'near on four years.'

'Four years?' exclaimed Billy in alarm. 'But I'll be old by then.'

Pete shrugged.

'I'm not stayin' here,' Billy's voice rose. 'I'm goin' home,' he cried. 'I'm goin'—'

'Shh!' Pete slapped a hand over his mouth. 'Don't let Mr B hear you,' he hissed, glancing nervously at the table where the sweepmaster sat drinking ale from a huge tankard. 'And don't start snivellin' neither,' he added. 'If there's one thing Mr B can't abide it's kids who snivel. Sends him ravin' mad, it does.'

'What's wrong with that brat?' shouted the sweepmaster, getting to his feet.

'Nothin', Mr B, nothin',' said Pete, hastily wiping away Billy's tears with his sleeve. 'He's just got a bit of bacon rind stuck in his throat.'

Clem had been casting anxious glances at the boys when her father wasn't looking and had seen Billy's tears. 'What's for puddin', Mum?' she asked.

'Your favourite, my treasure,' the woman said, beaming at her fondly. 'Gingerbread nuts.'

'Not biscuits again?' exclaimed Mr Bullock. 'We never get no plum duff nor apple pie no more.'

'That's cos Clem likes biscuits,' his wife scolded him.

'What? Oh . . . Oh right.' His coarse features softened into a smile. 'Then biscuits is what we'll have, if that's what my little darlin' wants,' he said, stroking his daughter's cheek. 'Though I don't know why she's so fond of them.'

'Cos they don't make a mess of a pocket like a lump of pie,' whispered Pete. And the other boys giggled and nudged each other.

'Right,' said Mr Bullock when dinner was over and the dishes stacked away. 'We got to make an early start tomorrow, so I'm goin' to get some sleep – but I'll just make sure everythin's closed up tight first,' he said, taking a large key out of his pocket and locking the front door. 'Don't want no one tryin' to run away, do we?' he chuckled malevolently, looking pointedly at Billy.

The little boy's shoulders sagged and he stifled a sob.

'Come on, my lovely, up to bed,' said Mr Bullock, holding out his arms to Clem as his wife extinguished the oil lamp and lit a candle. But as he lifted his daughter, her long skirt caught on the back of her chair revealing a big, ungainly boot, which hung like an anchor from her spindly leg.

The sight of a crippled man, woman or child in Victorian London was so commonplace that nobody paid any attention to a girl with a club foot. But Clem was clearly distressed, for she flushed scarlet, pulled down her skirt and mumbled, 'Dad!' in a hurt voice.

'I'm sorry, I'm sorry, my lovely,' he whispered, mortified that he had embarrassed her. 'But I don't think no one saw it.'

'Put me down, Dad, I've forgotten my sampler,' she said. 'Nah, you go on up. I'll get it.'

'But you don't need your sampler, Clem. You can't sew in bed.'

'I want it, Dad. Please.'

'Very well. And you lot,' the sweepmaster wagged a finger at the boys, 'I don't want to hear no noise,

you understand?' he said, climbing the steep, narrow stairs to the bedroom above. 'I hear one squeak and I'll take my belt to the lot of you.'

As soon as her father had disappeared Clem hobbled over to the boys.

'Him all right?' she said, bending down next to Billy.

'He will be,' said Pete.

'I got somethin' for you, littl'un,' she said. And reaching into the deep pockets of her apron she drew out some gingerbread nuts. 'Like them, do you?'

Billy had never tasted gingerbread nuts before and the look and smell of them were enticing, but he shook his head. 'Want to go home,' he whimpered.

'Have a biscuit. Go on, it'll make you feel better,' Clem urged him. 'Got some for you lot too,' she said, emptying her pockets.

'Oh, thanks, Clem,' said Pete. 'That's real kind of—'

'Shh!' she warned him. And clinging to the banister with both hands she clomped up the stairs to bed.

Pete, Dick and Harry ate their biscuits in silence, bending forward to lick up the crumbs from the floor, not caring that their feast included dirt and ashes.

'Don't you want yours?' asked Dick, eyeing Billy's biscuit hungrily.

'Nah.'

'Good. Give it here then.' And grabbing the gingerbread nut Dick was about to cram it into his mouth when Pete gave him a sharp slap on the ear.

'What d'you do that for?' Dick cried, aggrieved.

'You know why,' snapped Pete.

'Oh, all right.' And looking very sheepish Dick broke the biscuit into three and gave a piece to Pete and Harry.

'What'll we do now?' he whispered as they crawled closer to the fire, warming their bare feet and hands.

'Let's play peg-tops,' suggested Harry.

'Nah, marbles.'

'Nah, five stones.'

'Yeh, five stones!'

'Shh, keep your voices down, Lor's sake!' Pete admonished them. 'D'you know how to play five stones, Billy?'

'Yeh,' said Billy, who had watched his brothers play often enough.

'Right then, you start,' said Pete, pulling five small clay cubes from his pocket.

'Nah, I don't want to.'

'Oh, come on, nipper, it's no use glumpin',' said Dick as Billy gazed sadly into the fire. 'You just got to make the best of it, like the rest of us. Look at it this way, least you got a roof over your head.'

'But I already had one.'

'Well, now you got another one. Go on, start playin'.'

Billy picked up one of the cubes, threw it in the air and tried to catch it on the back of his hand while picking up a second cube. But the first cube kept falling off .

'Not much good, is he?' muttered Harry.

'We'll be here all night at this rate,' sighed Dick.

'It's cos I'm done up,' protested Billy.

'Yeh, you look dog-weary, you'd best go to sleep, nipper.'

Billy got up and began to climb the stairs.

'Nah, not up there, you stupe!' cried Pete. 'There's only one room up there and only one bed and all the Bullocks are in it,' he said, grabbing Billy and dragging him back down again. 'We all doss down here . . . And not in front of the fire,' he added, turning back to the game. 'Me, Dick and Harry have bagged them places.'

Billy curled up as close to the fire as he could, bringing his knees up to his chin to keep warm. He felt lonely without Jem and Ned beside him and fearful of what the morning would bring. Chimney sweeps with their bags of brushes on their backs were a common enough sight on the streets of London, but he had never given a thought to what they did or how they did it.

After a while the Mateys grew tired of their game of five stones and, stretching out in front of the fire, they settled down to sleep. But Billy was too nervous to sleep.

'Dick,' he whispered, nudging the boy next to him. 'Will *I* go up a chimney in the mornin'?'

'Yeh, course you will.'

'Is it a long way up?'

'A plaguy long way.'

'Oh . . .' Billy thought about this for a while then he nudged Dick awake again.

'Now what?' said Dick.

'Is it fun climbin' up a chimney?'

'Fun?' said the boy incredulously. '"Arry," he said, prodding him in the back, 'Billy wants to know if it's fun climbin' chimneys.'

'Oh yeh, it's a right laugh,' Harry snorted.

'Tell him what happened to you.'

'Nah, he doesn't want to hear . . .'

'Go on,' Dick urged him.

Harry sat up, tucked his knees under his chin, wrapped his arms around them and leaned towards the fire to get the last vestiges of warmth from its dying embers.

'It was years and years ago when I was just a little kid,' he said. 'I'd been up a couple of chimneys before and it'd all gone serene. Matter of fact, I thought it was a bit of a lark.'

Dick stared at him in disbelief. 'No kid, now?' he said.

'Anyway,' Harry went on, ignoring him, 'I had to do a job in a house in—'

'You with Mr B at the time, were you?' asked Dick.

'Look, if you're goin' to keep buttin' in . . .'

'All right, all right, no need to get snaggy.'

'As I was sayin',' continued Harry, glaring at Dick, 'I did this job in a house in a place called Swiss Cottage – that's out in the country,' he explained to Billy, who was listening intently, 'about a hundred miles from here. A bloke lived there with a couple of servants . . . Old?' he rolled his eyes. 'That bloke was so old another bone fell off every time he moved. *I mean it*,' he insisted as Dick laughed. 'You just had to look at him and he started crumblin'. So they kept the place real hot for him. Phew!' he whistled. 'Hot as hell it was cos they had the fires goin' day and night. They'd only just put them out before we got there. Course, they swore blind they'd done it ages before but,' he sighed, 'no use argufyin' with them. Mr B said, "Go on, 'Arry, get on with it," so I went up the chimney and . . .'

His voice faded away.

'And what was it like?' Dick prompted him.

'I only got up a bit of the way. The bricks were red hot. They were so hot they . . .'

Again he faltered.

'Show Billy what they did to you.'

Slowly Harry lifted up his shirt.

'Blimey!' breathed Billy, for the skin on the boy's back had puckered into a mass of ugly, purple whorls.

'My hands are the same,' said Harry, turning them palms up for Billy to see. 'And the bottom of my feet.'

'So did you burn to death?' whispered Billy.

'Course not, you stupe, else I wouldn't be here now, would I? I remember fallin' down the chimney, screamin' like to raise the dead, and one of the maids chucked a bucket of water over me and . . .' he shrugged, 'I don't remember no more. Mr B brought me back here at the double, and his missus wrapped

me tight in a blanket and she said I nearly croaked. Clem kept cryin' and huggin' me – that hurt,' he grimaced, 'but I didn't mind cos I knew she meant well – and when Mr B wanted to kick me out cos I wasn't no use to him no more, she wouldn't let him.'

'Clem's a crack article,' said Pete, who had been listening.

Harry and Dick nudged each other and sniggered.

'Has Clem been up a chimney?' asked Billy.

'Don't be daft, girls aren't sweeps,' said Pete. 'Anyway, Mr B wouldn't let her do nothin' like that. Apple of his eye, she is.'

'And Pete's,' muttered Dick. And he and Harry started sniggering again.

'Shut up, you two,' growled Pete, glowering at them.

'Tell Billy what happened first time *you* went up a chimney, Pete,' said Dick.

'Well . . .' Pete leaned back and folded his arms. 'I was doin' all right, got halfway up, then I slipped. I couldn't stop myself, I just kept slidin' and slidin'. Trouble was I tore so much skin off I looked like a side of beef when I hit the bottom. Mr B said he felt like chuckin' me in the oven for dinner.'

Dick and Harry laughed appreciatively, although they had heard the story — and the joke — many times.

'My brother wasn't so lucky,' continued Pete, his expression changing in an instant from jocularity to sorrow. 'Joe fell down and broke his neck. He was just about your age, Billy,' he said, resting his hand on the little boy's shoulder, 'and he looked just like you too, the spittin' image. The first time I clapped eyes on you I thought to myself, *Blow me down, it's Joe.*'

'Remember Tim,' said Dick, joining in Pete's sombre mood. 'He got stuck up the chimney and couldn't get down.'

'And Will got a load of soot in his lungs and near choked to death,' said Harry.

'And Fred . . .'

'Shut up!' shouted Mr Bullock from the top of the stairs. 'I hear another word out of you lot and you'll regret it.'

Billy crawled into a dark corner, buried his head in his hands and began to sob.

'Lor's sake, we won't get no sleep tonight at this rate,' complained Dick. 'What's wrong with him now?'

'Don't know. What's wrong, nipper?' said Pete. 'You got the collywobbles or somethin'?'

'I don't want to be a sweep,' wept the little boy. 'I want to go home, I want my mum.'

5

The Perkinskis were holding a council of war. Brothers, sisters, uncles, aunts and cousins had come from all over London in answer to Pa's urgent call and now they were crowded into the little courtyard at the end of Devil's Acre, listening to him with rapt attention.

Cries of disgust and outrage greeted his news that Billy had been kidnapped.

'He was out workin' with Jem and Ned at the time. But it wasn't their fault he was pinched,' Pa said as the boys hung their heads in shame. 'It was a right pea-souper and they got lost. It was just their bad luck to end up in St Giles.'

'*St Giles?*' There were gasps of horror.

'How did it happen?' asked Uncle Sid.

'Well, we were walkin' down this alleyway,' said Jem, 'and we couldn't see nothin', I couldn't hardly see my own nose, but we could hear all kinds of noises, grunts and growls like a load of wild animals—'

'I didn't hear nothin' like that,' said Ned.

'Howsomever,' said Jem, ignoring the interruption, 'we went on and all of a sudden this huge, hairy monster leaped out at me. Horrible it was, fire comin' out of its mouth and blood drippin' from its fangs and its skin lumpy and green like somebody'd been sick all over it and—'

'Pa, he's tellin' whoppers again,' protested Kate.

'Yeh, he is,' Ned agreed. 'It was just a cat. And it didn't leap out. He tripped over it.'

'Stow it, Jem,' said his father angrily. 'Your ma's near off her head with worry and she doesn't want to hear none of your giffle-gaffle. Another sappy word out of you and there'll be blood comin' from *your* fangs on account of my fist in your mouth.'

'To be honest, Pa, we don't know how it happened,' said Ned. 'One minute Billy was there, snivellin' the way he always does about bein' cold and hungry and wantin' to go home, and the next minute he'd gone, vanished into thin air. We kept lookin' for him but it was no use. The fog was so thick we thought we'd have to stay in St Giles all night . . .' There were more gasps of horror at this. 'But then we bumped into a couple of decent blokes,' Ned went on, 'and we told them as how we were lost and they brought us back here.'

'Gave me a terrible shock, it did,' said Ma. 'I haven't slept a wink since.'

'Don't take on, lovey,' said Cousin Annie, putting a comforting arm around her shoulders. 'We'll find the nipper.'

'But how?' wailed Ma.

'I reckon we should tell the police,' said Uncle Percy's son Bob.

At that all the Perkinskis fell silent and stared at the boy as if he'd made the most disgusting smell.

'*What* did he say?' Pa asked Uncle Percy, because he couldn't believe his own ears.

'I'm sorry, Bert,' said his brother, hanging his head in shame. 'His ma and me've tried to bring him up proper, but some kids just go off the rails. What can we do?' He raised his hands in a helpless gesture.

'Don't fret yourself, Percy,' said Pa. 'It was a mistake, wasn't it, son?' he said to Bob. 'A slip of the tongue.'

The boy, who by now was as red as a herring, mumbled that he was sorry, he didn't know what had come over him and he promised he'd never say such a stupid thing again.

'So what can we do to help, Uncle Bert?' said Bob's older brother, Sam, who had taken a day off from horse stealing when he received Pa's urgent message.

'I want you all to keep your ears flappin' and your eyeballs swivellin',' said Pa, 'cos somebody must know where Billy is.'

'We'll give you all the help we can, Bert,' Uncle Arthur reassured his brother. 'Just say the word.'

'That's uncommon generous of you, Arthur,' said Pa.

'To tell you the truth,' piped up Cousin Jenny, 'I'm wonderin' if it's the Terror that's got Bi—'

'Hold your jaw!' growled her husband. 'You know it's bad luck just sayin' that brute's name.'

'It's my opinion whoever swiped Billy did it for money,' said Cousin Maud. 'They'll be askin' for a ransom, you mark my words.'

'Nah,' Pa shook his head. 'Billy's not worth nothin' – not to nobody but us, I mean.'

'But just in case Maud's right, here's a start,' said Uncle Ben. And lifting Pa's hat off he put it on the table and threw a coin in it. 'Let me know if you need more, Bert,' he said as he left. The rest of the Perkinskis all followed his example, murmuring words of comfort as they filed out.

Pa waited till the last 'Goodbye' and 'Good luck' had floated back on the night air before picking up the hat.

'How much did we get, Pa?' said Jem.

'Must be a fair bit,' said Ned. 'There were forty of them . . .'

'Forty-four,' Kate corrected him.

'So if they all put in sixpence . . .' Pa started to count on his fingers.

'We got twenty-two shillin's,' said Kate.

'Well, it's nice to know I got such a generous family any rate,' said Pa, 'though I don't know if this'd be enough to get our Billy back,' he added, looking sadly at the pile of silver coins on the table.

At that Ma Perkinski covered her face with her shawl and rocked from side to side, groaning.

'Billy'll be all right, Ma, you see,' said Jem. 'We'll find him.'

'Nah, you won't,' said Pa. 'I don't want you and Ned doin' nothin' daft. D'you hear what I'm sayin'?'

'But, Pa . . .'

'I said d'you hear what I'm sayin', Jem?'

'Yeh, I hear,' said Jem, staring at the ground.

'This is a man's job, it's dangerous. You leave it to your uncles and me. We'll get Billy back sooner or later.'

6

Billy lay awake for a long time trying to think of ways to escape, but all the doors and windows were tightly shut and so at last he fell into a fitful sleep and dreamed he was home again, curled up between his brothers on the straw mattress in their caravan in Devil's Acre, scratching himself when a flea bit him or a bed bug sucked his blood.

An hour or so before dawn he woke up under a blanket of bodies.

'Shove over, Ned,' he said, pushing the boy next to him. 'Get off, Jem,' he grumbled, giving the boy on the other side a good kick.

There were mutterings and groans but neither boy moved.

'Oh, come on,' said Billy irritably, 'you lot deaf?' And he sat up.

The fire had gone out and the house was bitterly cold. The little boy looked around him, peering into the darkness, trying to make out where he was. It

was the smell that confused him. His parents' caravan smelt, of course. Ma had neither the time nor
the energy to clean it since she was out from dawn to
dusk trying to earn a few pennies, and the years of
accumulated dirt, grease and sweat had given it its
own particular odour, but the smell in Billy's nose
that morning was unfamiliar. There was a sharp,
acrid quality to it that stung his eyes and burned his
throat.

He turned to say something to the boy on his
right . . . But it wasn't Jem, who always slept with
his hat on, nor Ned, whose grimy hair stuck up
like a porcupine's quills. These were strange boys,
their clothes covered in black, foul-smelling
grime . . .

'Oh, crikey!' he gasped, suddenly realizing where
he was. 'Ma!' he cried, bursting into tears. 'Ma!'

'What's the matter with you?' Pete rolled over
and rubbed his eyes sleepily. 'Why you grizzlin'
again?'

'I don't . . . don't want to . . . don't want to go up
a chimney,' Billy sobbed.

'You'll have to, nipper. Mr B'll make you.'

'I'll run away. I'll . . .'

'Nah,' Pete shook his head. 'Ain't no use. Mr B or
one of his cronies'd catch you before you got fifty

yards and then he'd beat the livin' daylights out of you. Nah, you'd best stay here and do what he says.'

'But my pa'll come lookin' for me,' cried Billy. 'And my brothers and my . . .'

'Don't be daft,' Pete scoffed, 'this is St Giles. Even the crushers don't come here. If your pa and brothers was to come nosin' around they'd have their bellies ripped open and their gizzards spread all over the pavement before they could cry out. Nobody'd hear them, anyway, and nobody'd care. There are people murdered here every day, dozens of them . . . Blimey, who's that at this time of the mornin'?' he exclaimed as the front door reverberated to a loud and persistent knocking.

Billy's heart leaped. 'It's my pa,' he cried. 'I told you he'd come. I told you. I—'

'Shut that kid up!' growled Mr Bullock, lumbering down the stairs in his nightgown and cap with a heavy cosh in his hand. 'Stick him under the table, Pete, and if he makes so much as a squeak . . .'

He brandished the cosh at Billy. 'Dick, you hide behind the door and don't make a move till I give you the word. All right, Harry . . .' He nodded at the boy.

Harry opened the door a crack, but the next

moment it was thrown open, knocking him off his feet, and a burly man barged in complaining loudly about selfish people tucked up in their warm beds, who kept decent people like him waiting for hours and hours on a freezing doorstep.

'Gerry,' said Mr Bullock, putting down the cosh, 'what you doin' in St Giles?'

'Ah, well . . .' The man stopped ranting, took off his hat, placed it solemnly over his heart and said, 'I've come on account of our poor dear mother. It's my painful duty to inform you, George, that she has shuffled off this mortal coil.'

'She's done what?'

'Died.'

'Ah,' said Mr Bullock. 'Her heart, was it?'

'Nah, an oyster. It must have been a bit dodgy, George, cos after she'd eaten it she said, "Lawks, my belly don't arf ache," and then,' a tear trickled down his cheek, 'she kicked the bucket.'

'Gawd rest her soul,' said Mr Bullock, pulling off his nightcap and bending his head reverently. 'How much did she leave me?'

'Five quid and a chair – though to be honest the chair's not in the best of condition. It's only got three legs.'

'And what did she leave you, Gerry?' said Mrs

Bullock, who had joined them when she realized it was only her brother-in-law at the door.

'Just a few quid, Flo, and a chair.'

'And how many legs has *your* chair got?'

The man shuffled from foot to foot, doing his best not to catch her eye. 'Well, to be frank, Flo, to be quite frank . . .'

'Yeh?' Mrs Bullock crossed her arms.

'It's got four.'

'Just as I thought,' she huffed. 'My poor George always comes off second best. You were always her favourite, Gerry. Always made a fuss of you, she did. Spoilt you rotten.'

'Don't speak ill of the dead, Flo,' muttered her husband. 'When're they buryin' her, Gerry?'

'Day after tomorrow.'

'We must get movin' then, it'll take us the best part of two days to get to Guildford. Pete,' he turned to the boy, 'you and the Mateys get out on the street and make a bit of money while I'm away. And don't come back if you don't, you hear? I'm not stuffin' good vittals in the bellies of kids that don't earn their keep. I know, bein' a woman of breedin' what's used to actin' proper, you'd like to come with us to pay your respects to the dear departed, Flo,' he said to his wife, 'but I think my mum, may she rest in peace,

would agree it's more important you stay here to keep an eye on that little toerag,' he pointed at Billy, who was still under the table, 'in case he does a bunk.'

'Don't you fret yourself, Mr Bullock,' she said, glaring at Billy. 'Clem'n me'll watch him day'n night.'

7

Pa and his brothers and cousins and friends and neighbours set off at dawn every day to search for Billy, but though they combed London from one end to the other, plodding back weary and downcast at night, they did not find him.

'We started in St Giles,' said Pa. 'Nah, don't get fidgety, Liza,' he added as Ma expressed alarm, 'there were more'n forty of us, so they couldn't touch us, though we got plenty of dirty looks and worse. Of course, nobody we asked'd ever seen or heard of Billy, you'd think nobody never got nabbed in St Giles if you listened to them. Arthur and me agreed he'd probably been taken somewhere else – well, you don't steal a horse and hide it in your own yard, do you? So we all split up and went looking in other parts. A woman told me they saw a kid lookin' just like Billy in a soup kitchen near Whitechapel, then a bloke said he'd spent the night with him in a doss house in Battersea, then someone spotted him pushin' a coster barrow in Covent Garden . . .' Pa sighed and rubbed his aching feet, 'but it was never Billy. Never anythin' like Billy. To tell you the truth, I'm beginnin' to think . . .'

'Nah, don't say it, Bert,' his wife clutched his arm. 'Don't even think it. Billy's alive. I know he is. You got to keep lookin'.'

'Course we will, lovey, course we will,' said Pa, patting her hand comfortingly. But his expression was grim.

8

'You can make yourself useful, Billy,' said Mrs Bullock, handing him a broom. 'Go upstairs and sweep the bedroom. Proper, mind! Under the bed and behind the door. If I find any dust, even the smallest speck, there'll be no supper for you tonight.'

'And what can I do, Mum?' asked Clem.

'You can help me mend Pete's trousers, my ducky. Look at them, full of rips'n tears. I sometimes think he must drag himself down the street on his backside . . . Don't bang the broom on every step, Billy,' she scolded as he clambered up the steep stairs. 'Lift it up.'

Billy had never seen a bedroom before, not a proper one with a bed and a rack for hanging clothes and pictures on the walls and curtains on the windows . . . Window! He ran to it eagerly and fumbled with the latch, but Mrs Bullock must have heard him for she shouted, 'Come away from there, you little varmint! It's locked. ''Sides, you'd break your neck if you jumped.'

With a sigh Billy turned away from the window and for want of anything better to do, because he had no idea how to sweep a room and no desire to learn, he looked at the pictures on the walls, which were exceedingly dull, and examined the clothes on the rack, which were the family's Sunday best: Mr Bullock's suit, Mrs Bullock's shawl and bonnet, Clem's dress and pantaloons.

'Billy, are you workin'?' shouted Mrs Bullock.

'Course I am,' he shouted back, picking up the broom and banging it on the floor.

'Have you swept under the bed?'

'I'm doin' it.'

He looked at the bed longingly. It was a real one, with a big goosefeather mattress and pillows, not the bit of dirty cloth spread over a pile of straw that Billy shared with Jem and Ned in his parents' caravan, and it looked inviting, so inviting that the little boy couldn't resist climbing into it. Just for a minute, of course. Just to see how it felt . . .

9

'We got to do somethin', Ned,' said Jem. 'We got to go and find Billy.'

'But we can't. You promised Pa.'

'I didn't.'

'You did. He told you he didn't want you to do nothin', and you said yeh.'

'I did not. He asked if I'd heard what he was sayin' and I said yeh . . . Look, Pa's dead beat,' he went on quickly before Ned could point out the error in his argument. 'He's walked his trotters off lookin' for Billy. And if you're too lily-livered to help me find him, I'll go on my own.'

'I am not lily-livered,' exclaimed Ned angrily.

'So you're comin' with me?'

'Well, I . . .'

'Good. Let's go and see Gran.'

'Nah, we don't want Gran taggin' along. I seen slugs walkin' faster than her.'

'She's not comin' with us, you block'ead!'

'So what we goin' to see her for'

'Cos she's a witch, isn't she? She can do all kind of magic things, like seein' where Billy is.'

'Oh yeh?' Ned scoffed. 'If she's a witch, why'd she let old Ramsbottom nick her pearl brooch?'

'What d'you mean?' Jem frowned.

'If she's a witch she should've known what he was thinkin'. She should've known he was goin' to nick it.'

'Oh. Oh, well . . . er . . . well she did, only he walloped her one so she couldn't stop him.'

'I didn't know that,' protested Ned.

'Course you didn't. But I did,' said Jem, giving him a sly wink. 'I know everythin'.'

'I already offered my services to your father, but he said I was a silly witch and he didn't believe in all that whim-wham,' said the old woman huffily. 'And you don't neither, do you, Ned?' She glared at him. 'I know what you been sayin' to your brother about me.'

Ned swallowed hard, remembering how he'd mocked his grandmother. 'Crimes,' he whispered in Jem's ear, 'how does she know what I said?'

'I told you, she's a witch.'

'I am *not* a witch,' said Gran. 'I'm a seer. I can see

things far, far away. I can see through walls and doors too.'

'How d'you do that?'

'I do it with the help of my spirits, the souls of the dear departed. They come to me when I call them.'

'Could you give them a call now, Gran, and ask them where Billy is?'

'Nah, I got to do it at night when it's dark.'

'All right, we'll come back tonight.'

'Nah, I got a important customer comin' tonight.'

'But, Gran . . .'

'Jem, I got to make a livin'. I can't live on fresh air.'

'But, Gran . . .'

'Come back tomorrow night when it's dark . . . and Jem,' she caught his arm as he turned to go, 'don't tell no one, specially not your pa. He'll only laugh, and that'll make the spirits angry. And when they're angry they can turn very nasty.'

10

Billy fared rather well in the snug little house in St Giles while Mr Bullock was away. He had a warm place to sleep in front of the fire, until it went out, and for the first time in his life good food in his stomach and plenty of it. For this he had to thank Clem, who kept him well supplied with titbits when her mother wasn't looking. Indeed on one momentous occasion when Mrs Bullock was nattering with a neighbour on her doorstep Clem had given him a piece of pork pie.

Of the Mateys he saw little. Mindful of Mr Bullock's stern warning they were gone before dawn and did not return until late at night, too tired after a day stealing and begging for money on the streets to do anything other than swallow the scraps Mrs Bullock gave them and curl up in front of the fire for a few hours.

On the fifth night Mr Bullock returned, weary from his journey and ill-tempered about his inheritance.

'The chair Mum left me only had two legs. It couldn't even stand up,' he complained to his wife, 'and I had to pay two quid towards the cost of her funeral.'

'Never mind, my love, the boys've done well while you've been away.' She nodded at the Mateys, who had roused themselves from sleep to greet the sweepmaster. 'They made three guineas,' she said, putting the money in his outstretched hand.

'Three guineas?' Mr Bullock was impressed. 'I don't suppose you want to go back to sweepin' chimneys now, Pete?'

'I do,' said Pete with feeling. 'I'm fed up pickin' pockets. There's no fun in it. People make it too easy.'

'And what about him?' The sweepmaster pointed at Billy, who had hidden under the table in the hope Mr Bullock wouldn't notice him.

'He's been good as gold, hasn't he, Clem?' said Mrs Bullock.

Billy stared at the girl in dismay, fearing she would tell her father about his misdeeds. Without Clem's intervention he knew her mother would have thrashed him many a time, but always the girl was there to save him before the woman found out, hastily sweeping the floor when she discovered him fast asleep in the family bed, mopping up the oil when he knocked over the lamp, patiently taking her place at the back of the queue after he'd dropped the precious bucket of water they'd waited for for hours, rescuing the biscuit barrel he'd thrown on the fire, mistaking it for a log . . .

But Clem smiled sweetly, crossed her fingers behind her back and said, 'Yes, Mum, Billy's been good as gold.'

11

As night fell a thick fog blanketed the city, blocking out the moon and stars. Crouching low, Jem and Ned stole up the steps of their grandmother's caravan and tapped softly on the door.

The old woman opened it and peered round cautiously.

'It's all right, nobody's seen us. We can't hardly see ourselves in this pea-souper,' whispered Jem.

Gran beckoned them in, closed the door and pointed to a small table with three stools around it. 'Sit there and don't touch nothin',' she said, pushing Jem's hand away as he reached out to the bottles, jars and pots full of brightly coloured liquids and foul-smelling ointments that covered every shelf, ledge, nook and cranny.

'What we goin' to do, Gran?' he asked.

'You're not doin' nothin', son, just sittin' still and keepin' quiet while I contact my spirits.'

'What're the spirits like?' Ned asked nervously.

'Just like the livin', some are good and some are wicked. Some want to help me but others . . .' The old woman shuddered. 'I just hope we don't get none of the others tonight. And now I'm goin' to snuff out the candle.'

'Nah, Gran!' cried Ned in alarm. 'We don't have to sit in the dark, do we?'

'I told you it's got to be real dark for my spirits to come. Not a chink of light anywhere.' And she pinched the wick of the candle, plunging the caravan into inky blackness. 'Right, everyone hold hands and don't let go, no matter what happens. We're formin' a magic circle,' she said, reaching out to grasp the boys' hands, 'but if anyone breaks it, the evil spirits'll get in.'

'Crimes, Ned!' Jem grumbled. 'You don't have to hold that hard. You're near breakin' my fingers.'

'Quiet, both of you. I'm goin' to put myself into a trance.'

'What's a trance, Gran?'

'It's like bein' asleep only you're awake.'

'But how can you be asleep . . .?'

'Lawks a mercy, Jem, hold your jaw and let me get on,' snapped the old woman. And closing her eyes she began to rock back and forth, breathing slowly and deeply.

'Gran! Gran!' Jem tugged at her hand.

'Now what?'

'How will we know when the spirits're here?'

'They'll knock. I ask them questions and they knock on the table to answer.'

'But how . . .?'

'One more word from you, Jem, and you can find Billy yourself.'

'Sorry, Gran. I won't say nothin' more, promise.'

The old woman closed her eyes again and after a few minutes she began to groan, softly at first, then louder and louder. Ned squeezed his eyes tightly shut and tried to pretend he was a million miles away from the dark, creepy caravan with his grandmother swaying and howling like a soul in torment, but to his horror the table began to rise, wobbling at first, as if it were unsure, them moving higher and higher as if it were being pushed towards the ceiling.

'Well, I'll be jiggered!' breathed Jem.

'It's them, the spirits, they've c . . . come,' stammered Ned.

'Shh!'

'Hold on.' Ned clutched his brother with a sweaty hand. 'Hold on tight or they'll get us.'

'Shh!'

'Is there anybody there?' cried Gran in a strange,

sepulchral voice. 'I feel someone very close. Knock once if there's anybody there.'

Jem leaped up and Ned made a dive for the floor as a loud knock rang out.

'Thank you, spirit,' cried Gran. 'Who are you? Do I know you? Give one knock if you're a boy, two if you're a girl.'

Immediately two knocks rang out.

'Thank you, spirit. Give one knock if you're a . . .'

'Oh, come off it, Gran!' Kate's voice wafted through the door. 'I can't stand out here all night knockin'.'

The table fell to the floor with a dull thud.

'What d'you want, Kate?' snapped the old woman.

'Ma wants to know if you've seen the boys, cos their supper's ready.'

'Tell your ma I did see them but I can't see them now,' replied Gran quite truthfully.

'All right, you can light the candle, Jem. My spirits won't come back now,' she said when Kate had gone. 'I can't help you.'

'But you must, Gran, you must.'

'It's no use, son. All this messin' about's givin' them the jitters.'

'Please, Gran. We got to find Billy. You got to help us,' Jem pleaded.

'All right, I'll have one last try.' And she got up, took a box from a shelf, carefully drew out a shiny glass ball, and placed it in the middle of the table on a piece of black velvet cloth.

'What's that, Gran?'

'A crystal. I see things in it . . . Don't touch it, Jem. If you keep rubbin' your dirty fingers all over it I won't see nothin'.'

'What kind of things d'you see, Gran?'

'Sometimes I see things that have happened, sometimes things that're happenin' now, sometimes things that're goin' to happen. And sometimes they get all jumbled up, so I don't know where I am.'

'Can I have a look?' said Jem, peering over her shoulder.

'You won't see nothin' cos you don't have the gift like I have,' she said, pushing him back on his stool. 'It's somethin' you're born with, like second sight or . . . Oh!' she leaned forward eagerly, staring intently at the crystal.

'What? What can you see, Gran?'

'It's Billy,' she pointed. 'I see him quite clear. There he is.'

'Where, where?'

'He's gone.' She gave the crystal a quick wipe with the velvet cloth. 'Nah, there he is again. He's in a cart

99

with some other kids, climbin' boys by the look of them and . . . Oh, lawks a mercy!'

'What?'

'Here come a load of crushers.'

'Have they got him, they got Billy?'

'Nah, he's runnin', he's runnin' away . . . Now a man's got him, good lookin' fellow, I'm sure I seen him before somewhere.' The old woman leaned back, frowning. 'Now where was it . . .?'

'Never mind about him, Gran,' shouted Jem. 'What's Billy doin'?'

'Oh, poor little mite, he's in a horrible place now. It's cold and dark. And there's someone comin', someone . . . Stop breathin' on the crystal, Jem, you're makin' it all foggy so I can't see nothin' . . . Yeh, there he is, comin' through the door, but I can't see his face. That's funny . . .'

'What is?'

'The crystal's gone all dark, like it doesn't want me to see who it is.'

'Give it a shake, Gran.'

'Nah, it's clearin' now. I can see the man. He's turnin' round. He's turnin'. He's . . . Oh, my Gawd!' she shrieked.

'What? What can you see?'

'That face! That face!' The old woman turned away and covered her eyes with trembling hands.

'Who is it?'

'I can't . . . I can't look at it.'

'Gran . . .?'

'It's too horrible.'

'But who is it?' Jem was so beside himself it was all he could do not to grab his grandmother by the shoulders and shake the answer out of her. He reached out for the crystal but she snatched it away.

'Nah, don't look,' she said, throwing the cloth over it. 'It'd give you nightmares.'

'But who was it, Gran? Who did you see?'

'Jim Rippen.'

'Jim . . .?'

'The most dangerous man in London,' the old woman whispered, looking over her shoulder fearfully as if she half expected him to be standing there. 'They call him the the Terror.'

'The Terror?' exclaimed Ned. 'Every time we do somethin' wrong Ma says the Terror'll get us. But she won't tell us nothin' about him. What's he like, Gran?'

'I tell you, son, there's no greater villain in the whole world. Him and his lot go all over town snatchin' little kids like Billy from the street. Then he starves them so's they stay nice and thin so's they can get up chimneys and earn him a pile of money. But when they grow too big and he can't send them up chimneys no more he slits their throats and chucks them in the river. He's murdered hundreds'n hundreds of kids, so they do say. And not just kids neither.'

'And you reckon he's got Billy, Gran?'

Tears welled up in the old woman's eyes. 'Yeh, he's got poor little Billy. No doubt about it.'

'Then we got to go and get him back.'

'You won't never get him back. Once the Terror gets you, you're . . .' Gran hesitated.

'You mean he's . . .?' Jem drew a finger across his throat.

She nodded. 'You'd best forget Billy, son.'

'But he's not dead yet, is he, Gran?'

She shook her head. 'But he will be. Nobody gets away from the Terror. Nobody.'

12

Billy woke at dawn, screaming.

'Oh Lor', now what?' grumbled Pete.

'I dreamed I was up a ch . . . chimney and I was b . . . burnin' and . . . and then I fell down and b . . . broke my . . .'

'Don't be daft, littl'un, you'll be all right, you see. You'll . . . Oy, watch out, here comes Mr B.' Pete's voice dropped to a whisper as the sweepmaster clumped down the stairs followed by his wife. 'And stop snivellin', Lor's sake,' he scolded the boy, scrubbing at his tear-stained face with the edge of his coat. 'I keep tellin' you he can't abide squally kids.'

'Get up, you lot,' the man shouted, kicking Dick and Harry awake. 'Get that fire lit.'

Yawning and scratching, the boys swept the grate clear of ashes and built up a pyre of paper, sticks and coal. While Mr Bullock set a kettle on to boil, his wife hung strips of bacon from a beam over the fire and cracked a dozen eggs into a sizzling pan.

'There's your grub,' she said to the sweep boys, putting on the floor a dish of half-eaten potatoes, the tough outer skin of an onion, dried-up tripe and hard dumplings in cold, congealed gravy.

'Eat it quick,' grunted Mr Bullock, ramming a wedge of fresh, crusty bread into his mouth. 'We got a real big job on today, the Earl of Clarendon's residence in Belgravia.'

The boys whistled and clapped appreciatively.

'Should bring us in a pretty penny or two,' said Pete.

'Where's Belgravy?' asked Billy.

'West of here, the other side of Green Park. It's where all the rich live.'

'I'm not goin' up the Oil's chimney, am I?' Billy asked in a small voice.

'Course you are. And fallin' down it,' said Dick. And he and Harry burst out laughing.

Billy's lower lip began to tremble, but Pete gave him a jab in the ribs and a warning look. 'Right, let's get goin', Mateys,' he said, wiping his mouth on his soot-blackened sleeves and pulling on a grimy cap. 'All hands to the sacks!'

The boys clambered down a flight of stairs to a dark cellar where piles of black, oily sacks used to carry the soot away were stacked almost to the ceil-

ing. Billy struggled up with as many as he could carry and put them in the back of a cart waiting at the kerb, but they were heavy and several times he fell, grazing his hands and knees.

It was still dark, but the fog had lifted and the day promised to be bright and clear. Billy stopped by the cart and looked about him. He was in a typical street in the Rookeries. Down the centre ran a drain clogged with rubbish, manure and the maggot-ridden bodies of dead dogs, cats and rats. The stench was overwhelming, but Billy was so used to it he barely noticed. Above him washing hung from every window so that the street appeared to be festooned with a grey bunting of vests and drawers and combinations, most of them so full of rips and holes it was impossible to tell whether they were clothes or cleaning rags.

Small children, many of them younger than Billy, were already up and about, searching the pavements for cigar ends, buttons, a shoe buckle, a piece of rope or string – anything they could sell to buy some bread or a mug of milk.

When all the sacks were loaded, Pete lifted Billy into the cart.

'All square, Mateys?' shouted Mr Bullock.

'All serene, guv!'

'Gerrup then, Dolly!'

The sweepmaster flicked his whip lightly at the mare's back, and as the cart lurched forward Billy noticed there was a broom nailed over the door of the house to show that the family were chimney sweeps.

The next moment the window above it slid open and Clem appeared with the remains of the crusty loaf in her hand. Pete stood up, his hands out-stretched, and she let it fall. With a huge grin the boy caught it and blew her a kiss.

'What you doin'?' shouted the sweepmaster over his shoulder.

'Just checkin' the sacks, Mr B.'

'Pete's spoony on Clem, always has been,' Dick whispered in Billy's ear. 'He wants to marry her — when he's a bit bigger, of course. I reckon Mr B and his missus know but they don't mind cos they got no son of their own, so when Mr B drops off the hook Pete'll take over the business. He'll be a good sweep-master,' he nodded approvingly, 'the best. Not like *him*.' He glanced at Mr Bullock, who was cursing and laying his whip on the urchins who ran up to the cart, begging for food and money.

Pete divided the loaf into four, with a slightly larger portion for himself — 'Cos I'm the leader,' he said, defying anyone to contradict him. Then, raising his voice over the grinding screech of the wooden wheels on the rough cobblestones, Pete explained to Billy what he would have to do when they reached the Earl of Clarendon's.

'You got to climb to the top of the chimney, take your brush like this,' he picked up a large, circular brush with a long handle, 'and sweep off all the soot as you climb back down. But you got to do it fast, cos people want us out of their houses plaguy quick . . . Watch out!' he warned as a woman emptied a chamber pot from an upstairs window with a cry of, 'Gardy loo!'

'Now to the real important part.' Pete put an arm around Billy's shoulder and drew him closer. 'On your way down the chimney you got to look in all the rooms and remember what's in them, like nice bits of silver, so's we can go back later and do the job on them.'

He winked knowingly at Billy.

'You mean we go back and clean them?' said Billy, who'd often seen Gran Perkinski spitting on her wedding ring and polishing it with her sleeve.

'Oh, crimes, where you been all your life?' Pete sighed. 'I mean we go back and arf-inch the stuff. We take it off their hands,' he explained, as Billy looked

at him blankly. 'We lift it, pinch it. Course we don't do it straightway or it'd look a bit fishy like. Nah, we wait a couple of weeks and then me and the other Mateys go back with Mr B and nick it all. This chimney sweepin' lark's just a cover.'

'Jem'd be uncommon good at that,' said Billy proudly. 'Jem could nick the tail off a donkey.'

'Who's Jem?'

'My brother. And I got another brother called Ned and a sister and . . .' Billy's eyes began to fill with tears as he thought of his family.

'Don't start that again,' hissed Pete, slapping a hand over Billy's trembling mouth to silence him, 'else you'll get us all in trouble.'

13

Billy crouched in the back of the sweepmaster's cart and watched the streets of London slowly come to life.

Drunken men and women lurched from one lamp-post to the next or snored noisily in dark doorways, while the homeless grubbed in the piles of rubbish for something to eat. And everywhere there were children even dirtier and more ragged than Billy and the Mateys, begging or looking for some handy pockets to pick.

After a while the mean, overcrowded streets of the slums receded and Dolly trotted briskly along the main thoroughfares of the capital. Herds of cattle and pigs plodded towards the market in Smithfields, tired and hungry after their long journey from farms far away. Flocks of geese and turkeys cackled along behind them, frightened by the noise and confusion.

Many people were already at work or on their

way to work — cabbies on the lookout for early fares, washerwomen with baskets of laundry on their heads, men staggering under the weight of pails of milk suspended from a wooden yoke across their shoulders, girls carrying heavy baskets of fruit, flowers and herbs, dressmakers hurrying to the sweatshops in the city where they worked from dawn till dusk with no breaks for food or rest. And on every street corner stood a man or boy urging people to buy a morning paper, singing out, '*Times!*' '*Chron!*' '*Herald!*'

Gradually the Mateys left the noisy workaday world behind them and arrived in Belgravia, one of the smartest areas of London, where all was tranquil. Tall, elegant houses with impressive front doors and gleaming bay windows looked on to tree-lined squares where, later in the day, uniformed nannies would push perambulators, with small children walking sedately alongside, the boys in sailor suits or blouses with lace collars and short skirts with frilly knickers to the knees, the girls dressed as miniature versions of their mothers in full skirts and lace-edged pantaloons and large hats weighed down with flowers and ribbons.

Footmen in gold-braided livery with buckled shoes and larded, powdered hair helped elegant men and women from carriages, many of which had coats of arms emblazoned on their doors.

Two maids in long black dresses and white starched aprons and caps were hovering in the area doorway of the Earl of Clarendon's residence, waiting for the young sweeps to arrive.

'Mornin', Mr Jones,' they called out when they saw the cart.

'Mornin' ladies,' said the sweepmaster, doffing his cap.

'Jones?' Billy frowned. 'His name isn't Jones. It's Bul—'

Pete slapped a hand over his mouth.

'He's Mr Jones to them people,' he whispered. 'And you keep quiet about it, nipper. The less they know about us the better.'

'Quick as you can, please, Mr Jones,' said one of the maids. 'Her Ladyship wants you out of the house before she wakes up.'

'I got the fastest climbin' boys in London, miss,' said Mr Bullock. 'Right, you lot, look sharp!' he bellowed at the Mateys. 'And don't stand there gawpin', Billy, or I'll tan the skin off your back and sell it for leather.'

Billy cringed and hid behind Pete.

'Look at them sappy girls,' Pete muttered,

pointing to the maids, who were giggling and nudging each other. 'They love it when sweep-masters get nasty. They think it's funny,' he said sourly.

'You two, stop jabberin'!' barked Mr Bullock, advancing on Pete and Billy with his whip held high.

The two of them scuttled down the area steps into a large kitchen where a stern-looking woman glared at them and said, 'Now follow me. And don't touch anything, you understand?' as she led the way up a narrow staircase into the main hall.

'Who's that?' whispered Billy. 'She the Oil of Clarendon's missus?'

'Don't be daft, she's his housekeeper. And a right old battleaxe too. She's got a tongue in her head sharp as a razor – so watch out.'

Billy had never been in a grand house like the Earl of Clarendon's, and although all the carpets and fur-niture in the reception rooms had been well covered with paper and dust sheets to protect them from soot, he had never seen, never imagined such ornate ceilings, such beautiful marble statues and glittering chandeliers. He stood and gazed about him in won-derment, quite forgetting his fear for the moment.

'Just like Buckin'ham Palace, eh?' whispered Pete, creeping up behind him.

Billy's eyes opened wide. 'You been to Buckin'ham Palace, Pete?'

'Course I have,' the boy laughed. 'The Queen has us over to tea every Sunday afternoon. Real nice to us Mateys, she is.'

'Oh, Pete,' sighed Billy, 'could I go with you next time? I'd really like to meet the old girl.'

'Oy!' shouted Mr Bullock. 'Get movin'. You're not here to admire the scenery, you lazy little faggots.'

'Quite right, Mr Jones,' said the housekeeper, nodding approval.

'Now remember what you got to do,' said Pete, as he and Billy followed her into a room with a large, ornate fireplace.

'Climb right up to the top of the chimney,' said Billy, 'get my brush out and . . .'

Pete looked furtively over his shoulder and whispered, 'I mean about keepin' your eyes skinned for "you know what".'

'Oh, yeh.' Billy nodded. 'You mean I got to look for silver and stuff for us to nick.'

'Shh!' Pete clapped his hand over the little boy's mouth.

'What did he say?' said the housekeeper sharply.

'He didn't say nothin', missus.'

'I could have sworn I heard him say "nick".'

'Nah, he said he was feelin' a bit sick.'

'For goodness' sake, boy,' she gave Billy a push, 'stop whining. Get up the chimney and quick about it.'

Billy crouched in the huge fireplace and looked up fearfully.

'It's . . . It's very dark,' he said in a trembling voice. 'I can't see nothin'.'

'That's cos there's nothin' to see,' said Pete. 'Pull your cap well down and roll your trousers up high as you can.'

'And there's no ladder. You said there was.'

'Well, I forgot to mention that some chimneys don't have ladders,' Pete shrugged. 'You just got to kind of wedge yourself in and wriggle up. It's easy. Honest.'

'But supposin' I fall down?' said Billy, his eyes filling with tears.

'Nah, you won't. And if you get tired you can stop for a bit and sit on one of the ledges.'

'But supposin' . . .?'

'If that boy isn't up the chimney by the time I get back,' snapped the housekeeper, 'I'm going to get someone else to do the job.'

'Go on, Billy. Please,' pleaded Pete as she stormed

out of the room. 'If we don't do this job right, Mr B'll beat us all black and blue.'

'Pete . . .' Billy clung to his arm. 'Come up with me.'

'I can't, nipper. I'm too big. I'd get stuck. But I'll be here at the bottom in case you fall.'

'But you said I wouldn't fall. You said . . .'

Billy squeezed his eyes tightly shut and screwed up his face, but before he could start crying again Pete whispered, 'It don't matter if you fall cos I'll catch you. You won't hurt yourself . . . Oh, Lor', that old biddy's comin' back. Get goin', Billy.'

'Pete, if I fall . . .'

'I'll catch you, like I said.'

'Promise?' said Billy doubtfully.

'Course I do. Now go on, up you go.'

Billy gave a deep sigh and, grasping his brush, he wedged himself into the chimney, as Pete had told him, and slowly began to work his way up into the darkness.

14

Pa refused to believe that the Terror had kidnapped Billy.

'It isn't that he wouldn't,' he explained to Jem and Ned, ''cos he'd kidnap Queen Victoria herself if he thought she'd be any good at sweepin' chimneys. But take it from me, Gran was fakin' it.'

'But, Pa, the table . . .'

'Gran was liftin' the table with her knees. I seen her do it myself.'

'And she saw Billy in her crystal and . . .'

'Crystal,' scoffed Pa. 'It's just a bit of glass.' And emptying his beer tankard in one gulp he tipped it upside down and squinted at the bottom. 'Lawks a mercy!' he cried, mimicking the old woman's croaky voice, 'I can see a cow flyin' over the moon.'

'But Pa, Gran was . . .'

'Makin' it up, Jem. Now I'm not tellin' you again,' he said sternly, 'stay out of this, the pair of you. You start interferin' and you'll end up in worse trouble than Billy.'

'Where does the Terror live?' Jem asked Uncle Arthur.

'He's got rooms at the George 'n Dragon just off Walworth High Street. He's a sweepmaster but he's got a nice little sideline goin' with the dog-and-rat sport, so I do hear.'

'What's that?'

'He puts vicious fightin' dogs in the ring with a load of rats, and everyone bets on which dog is goin' to kill the most. Very popular, it is. People come from miles around to . . . Here,' Uncle Arthur stopped, 'what d'you want to know about the Terror for?'

'Cos he's got Billy.'

'Who told you that?'

'A little bird,' said Jem, who knew his uncle would be as scathing of Gran's psychic powers as his father.

'Well, you take it from *this* little bird,' said Uncle Arthur, pointing at himself, 'if the Terror's got Billy, there's nothin' you nor me can do about it. Don't go nowhere near that fiend or you'll end up dead.'

*

'Ever heard of the Terror?' Jem asked Cousin Annie.

'Who hasn't?' she breathed, her eyes opening wide with fear. 'He's a sweepmaster, murdered Lor' knows how many climbin' boys. Crushers too. Only they can't prove nothin' against him. Uncommon clever, he is, clever as Old Nick himself. In fact,' her eyes darted back and forth as if she feared the Terror would leap out at her at any moment, 'some people think he *is* the devil, come back to earth to torment us.'

'Where is Walworth, Annie?'

She narrowed her eyes. 'You plannin' to go there or somethin'?'

'Course not,' lied Jem, putting on an expression of pained innocence. 'It's just that I've heard a lot about it.'

'It's on the other side of the river. You go over Waterloo Bridge, turn left and then . . .' She hesitated. 'You sure you're not plannin' to go there?'

'The Terror's got Billy,' Ned blurted out before Jem could stop him.

Cousin Annie recoiled in horror.

'Well, if he's got Billy the poor little wretch's good as dead. The Terror's probably eaten him . . . I'm not jokin',' she scolded, as Jem scoffed openly. 'I do hear as how he eats human flesh like the rest of us eat a bit of pork or chicken. It's disgustin', disgustin!' She shook her head in horror. 'That man should be strung up.'

15

Billy wriggled a few yards up the chimney and stopped.

'What's wrong?' demanded Pete.

'It's so dark, I can't see where I'm goin',' he whined.

'It'll get better as you go up,' lied Pete. 'For Lor's sake move, Billy, or we'll be in trouble with that dratted housekeeper.'

'What's happenin?' said Mr Bullock, coming into the room at that moment. 'Billy at the top yet?'

'Nah. He won't move, Mr B.'

'Reckon we'll have to give him a bit of encouragement then. Billy!' he shouted. 'We're goin' to get a nice big fire goin' in the grate. Look . . .' He lit a match. 'If you don't get up that chimney plaguy quick you'll be burned alive.'

'Nah, don't, don't!' screamed the little boy.

'Then start climbin'.'

'But . . .'

Way below another match flared.

'I'm goin' up,' Billy cried out in alarm. 'Don't burn me, guv, I'm goin' up.' And he eased himself up the chimney, pressing his back against the wall on one side and scorching his bare feet on the other, dislodging great clumps of soot, which fell on his face and filled his mouth. He gasped and spat out the vile stuff. The taste of it made him feel so sick that after a few mouthfuls he learned to keep his cap well down and his mouth tightly shut, as Pete had told him.

Up and up he went, pausing every so often to try and cool his blistered hands and feet. Once he missed his footing and nearly fell. 'Ma!' he cried. 'Ma!' And he clambered on to a ledge, sobbing.

At last he noticed it was getting lighter and there was a patch of blue sky above him. Elated at the prospect of getting out of the hot, dark chimney he clambered up the last few feet and, peering over the edge, let out a gasp of surprise. It seemed as if the whole of London was spread before him – on one side the River Thames, on the other hundreds of roofs stretching into the distance. And when he swivelled his head round he could see green fields and orchards behind him.

With a sigh of relief, he stepped out of the

chimney and perched on the edge. Directly below him was the square. He'd never seen trees or hansom cabs or people from above before and he was so excited he began to shout, 'Hey, I'm up here! I'm on top of the world! I'm . . .'

Suddenly he lost his balance, fell off the chimney and began to slither down the steeply sloping roof. There was a gasp of horror from the people who had gathered in the square below. Down and down he went and for one awful moment it looked as if he'd end up splattered all over the pavement, but just as he reached the edge of the roof he made a wild grab for a drainpipe and hung on.

'Fetch a ladder!' shouted someone.

'Get the fire brigade!'

'Don't look down, son!'

Billy clung to the drainpipe until he'd got his breath back, then, with pounding heart, he slowly edged his way up the roof again, using his hands and bare feet like an agile monkey, until he reached the chimney.

There was a tremendous cheer from the crowd and cries of, 'Well done, lad!'

Billy could see Mr Bullock and the two maids and he waved his brush at them. The maids laughed and waved back, but he could tell the sweepmaster wasn't pleased from the way he kept shaking his fist at him.

With a farewell wave, Billy lowered himself back into the chimney and began to climb down, brushing and sweeping furiously as he went so that he sent up great clouds of soot that engulfed him.

16

'We'll go tomorrow mornin',' said Jem. 'We'll catch some rats and take them to the George 'n Dragon and tell the Terror we got some nice little rodents for his dog-and-rat sport. So he'll buy the rats and then he'll take a look at us and think, Lor', love a duck, here's a nice couple of sweeps for my collection and before you can say kidnap we'll be inside and we'll find Billy.'

'Oh, that's real clever, that is. So then the Terror'll have all three of us,' jeered Ned. 'Nah, thanks. I don't want to end up on his plate.'

'Don't be daft. Cousin Annie only said that about him eatin' people to try and stop us goin' to see him.'

'But what'll we do when we find Billy?'

'Rescue him, of course.'

'How?'

'I'll think of somethin'.'

17

Finding his way up the chimney had been hard for Billy, but going down was even worse. It seemed to bend and twist, and other chimneys joined it, so that in the pitchy-blackness he got lost.

Climbing down what he thought was the right chimney he found himself in the fireplace of a beautiful room, in the centre of which stood a four-poster bed surrounded by silk drapes and covered with a richly embroidered counterpane. In the bed, fast asleep, was a lady wearing a frilly nightcap over her greying hair.

Billy crept out of the fireplace and stole across the room, stroking the fine furs and satin dresses that hung in the wardrobes, feeling the damask curtains, running his hands over the velvet chairs and silk cushions until there was nothing in the room that wasn't liberally covered with sooty marks.

A heart-shaped dressing table stood in the window bay, its surface covered with an assortment

of fine silver-backed brushes, crystal glasses and lac-
quered boxes containing creams and perfumes.

Billy picked up one of the bottles, pulled out the
stopper and sniffed it. At that moment he was aware
of a movement and looking up he saw a sooty monster with bright blue eyes staring at him intently. The
boy was so frightened he didn't realize the monster
was his own reflection in the mirror, and in his haste
to get away he stumbled over the stool and thudded
to the floor with a loud 'Ouch!'. The perfume bottle
he'd been holding fell out of his hand, tipping its
contents all over him.

Startled out of her sleep, the lady in bed sat
up and when she saw Billy she drew the satin
sheets around her shoulders and screamed, 'Help!
Help!'

Billy scrambled to his feet and ran towards the
fireplace, but before he could get there the door
burst open and a large, red-faced man in a dressing
gown and matching nightcap rushed in carrying a
poker, which he brandished menacingly.

'What the deuce . . .?' cried the Earl of Clarendon
when he saw Billy.

Scuttling across the white carpet, which by then
was beginning to look very grey from his footprints,
the little boy began to climb back up the chimney.

'Stop him! Stop him!' screeched the Countess of Clarendon.

'Don't worry, m'dear, I've got the thieving little brat,' said the Earl. And he lunged at Billy and grabbed his foot.

Billy wedged himself in the chimney as firmly as he could, but the Earl yanked at his foot and tried to pull him back, so that the boy bobbed up and down like a coiled spring, dislodging great clouds of soot, which swirled about the room, settling on the furniture and curtains and the Earl and his hysterical wife.

Realizing that he would never get up the chimney unless he dragged the Earl with him, Billy abruptly changed tactics. He jumped down, twisted his foot out of the man's grasp and charged at his knees. The Earl, taken by surprise, fell heavily, cracking his head on the fender surrounding the fireplace.

'Murder!' shrieked the Countess, leaping out of bed. 'Murder!'

Billy rushed out of the room, colliding with the lady's maid in the corridor, ran down the stairs, crashing into a footman who was bringing up a breakfast tray, bowled over the housekeeper and shot across the hall, leaving a trail of devastation and black footprints behind him.

The Earl bellowed, the Countess fainted, the lady's maid wept, the footman swore, the housekeeper had hysterics and above it all Billy could hear Mr Bullock roaring, 'Stop, you little bugger! Stop or I'll . . . I'll . . .!' But words failed him.

It was Pete who finally caught Billy, stopping him in his headlong flight down the front steps and bundling him into the cart waiting at the kerb.

'I'd lay low if I was you, nipper,' he warned, throwing some sacks over Billy to hide him. 'You're in a lot of trouble and . . . Phew!' he backed away in disgust, 'You don't half stink as well.'

'I knocked a bottle over,' explained Billy. 'It was in that old crone's room. The stuff went all over me.'

'Oh, Lor',' groaned Pete, 'that'll be her scent. It'll cost us a pretty penny. Stay there a kick and I'll go and see what the damage is.'

The damage, when Pete reappeared some time later, was ten guineas to cover broken glass and ornaments in the Countess's bedroom and one guinea to replace a bottle of French perfume.

'The Earl says we're never to darken his floors again,' said Pete. 'And . . . Look out, here comes Mr B. Get back under the sacks, Billy, or he'll beat you all to pieces.'

'Where is he? Where is that brainless little faggot?'

bellowed the sweepmaster, flailing at the air with his whip. 'Let me get my hands on him!'

'It wasn't his fault, guv,' said Pete, standing in front of the sacks so that the man couldn't see them shaking.

'Wasn't his fault? He near killed the Earl and gave his missus a heart attack. He wrecked their house. He . . .'

'It's cos he got lost on the way down, Mr B. He didn't do it deliberate.'

'Yeh, give him a chance, guv, he's only a nipper,' Dick urged him.

'And it was his first time,' added Harry.

The sweepmaster glared at them, clenching and unclenching his fists. 'All right,' he said at length. 'All right, I'll let him off . But I'm tellin' you now if that kid makes a mess of the next job I'll rip open his belly and use his guts for a washin' line, see if I don't!'

18

Jem and Ned were up well before dawn the next morning. Jem had very little idea where Walworth was, apart from being south of the river, but he fancied it was a long way off, so they would need plenty of time to get there and back again before nightfall.

'Keep quiet,' he admonished his brother as they slid out of their small bed, 'or you'll wake Pa. And if he finds out where we're goin', we're in trouble.'

They dressed quickly, Jem in his tailcoat, breeches and spats, Ned in overalls with rips and tears in revealing places and a pair of boots several sizes too big for him held together with bits of string.

'Ready?' whispered Jem.

'Nah, wait,' said Ned. 'I want somethin' to eat first.'

'We haven't got time.'

'I'm not goin' all the way to Walworth without . . .'

'Shh!' Jem put a finger to his lips and pointed at

Pa, who stopped snoring for a moment and stirred in his sleep. 'Look in there,' he pointed at the old orange box Ma used for storing what little food she had.

'There's only this.' Ned held up a small loaf of bread.

'That'll do,' said Jem, grabbing it from him.

'But we can't take it,' said Ned, horrified.

'Why not?'

''Cos it's Pa's breakfast.'

'So you don't want none then?'

Ned looked uneasily at his father. 'All right,' he said, holding out his hand.

'Right, now come on!'

'Where you two goin'?' said Kate, lifting her head and peering at them sleepily.

'We . . . er . . . we're just goin' out to look for Ned's catapult.'

'What, in the middle of the night?'

'He's so worried about it he can't sleep.'

'Oh yeh? That sounds like one of your whackers to me, Jem. And what are you doin' with that loaf? You know it's Pa's. Give me some of it, or I'll wake him up,' she added slyly.

Grumbling about how greedy girls were, Jem broke a piece off the loaf and handed it to his sister, who quickly devoured it and buried her head in the straw mattress again.

'Ta-ta, Kate,' whispered Jem, bending over her and giving her a quick peck on the cheek.

'Get off!' She sprang up, scrubbing her cheek vigorously. 'What'd you do that for?'

'You off your chump?' demanded Ned as Jem closed the door of the caravan softly behind them. 'Kissin' Kate?'

'I was just thankin' her.'

'For what?'

'This,' said Jem, holding up a penny. 'She always keeps money under her mattress. We'll need it to get across Waterloo Bridge.'

It was just before six o'clock on a cold, dark, winter's morning when the two boys crept out of the yard, each carrying a sack, which they intended to fill with rats.

Now there was a desperate shortage of many things in Devil's Acre, like money, food, warmth, light, water, but no shortage whatsoever of rats. The streets, houses and yards teemed with them. They ran along the walls, swarmed in and out of the drains and rooted through the piles of rubbish and manure. But catching them was not as easy as the boys had thought.

'Why is it when I'm sittin' in the gutter mindin' my own business the varmints are runnin' all over me, up one leg and down the other,' complained Jem. 'But when I want one, I can't seem to . . .' he made a lunge at a rat, missed it and fell heavily . . . 'catch it.'

'We'll be here all day this rate,' said Ned.

'I know what, we'll put some food down and wait for them to come for it, then nab them.'

'Yeh, that's a good idea.'

'Go on, then.'

'Go on, what?'

'Put some food down.'

'I'm not givin' them any of my bread. Why don't you give them some of yours?'

'Cos it was my clever idea.'

'Then you do it, clever!'

'Oh, all right,' grumbled Jem. And breaking off a tiny piece of crust, he crumbled it on to the pavement.

'There'll be hundreds of them when they get a whiff of that,' he said. 'I'll hold the sack and you pick them up by their tails and put them in.'

'Why don't *you* pick them up and put them in?' demanded Ned.

'Cos I don't see why I should do everythin'. I

already gave them half my breakfast, isn't that enough?'

Muttering under his breath about the unfairness of it all and the rottenness of brothers, Ned crouched in the gutter, waiting for the rats to take the bait while Jem stood by with a sack at the ready.

And they waited. And waited.

'Move away a bit, Ned,' suggested Jem. 'You're scarifyin' them.'

Ned edged away from the bait and a large rat, braver or hungrier than the others, scuttled towards it and began to nibble.

'Now!' shouted Jem.

Ned leaped forward and made a grab for it. The rat, startled, sank its sharp yellow teeth into the boy's finger and made off down the sewer.

'You shouldn't have let it go,' grumbled Jem as Ned yelled and hopped about in pain. 'And it's eaten all my bread too.'

'You catch them then,' said Ned, aggrieved. 'That varminty thing's nearly bitten my finger clean off.'

'Gave you quite a nip, didn't it?' said Jem, examining the wound. 'I only hope you don't die of it.'

'What d'you mean?'

'You can get canker from a rat bite, cos they're horrible infectious.'

'Canker?'

'Yeh. Your finger'll go all green and slimy and then it'll drop off.'

Ned gulped. 'Why didn't you tell me that before? Supposin' I do die?'

'Nah, I was only kiddin', you won't die. You're a lot dirtier than them rats. In fact, I shouldn't be surprised if that rat isn't dead itself after bitin' you.'

'Well, I'm not catchin' no more,' pouted Ned, sucking his finger.

'Tell you what,' said Jem, 'we'll get some cats and put them in the sack instead. They'll be much easier to catch. Anybody can catch a cat. Even you.'

'But the Terror doesn't want cats, he wants rats.'

'I don't see why he couldn't have a dog and cat sport. Dogs like chasin' cats just as much as rats.'

'But . . .'

'You got a better idea?' demanded Jem irritably.

'Nah.'

'Then stop argufyin'.'

So the two boys set about catching some of the wild, half-starved moggies that haunted the alleys and courtyards around Devil's Acre. But for some reason not one of them wanted to go to Walworth in a sack that morning, although all of them seemed to be in the mood for hissing and scratching furiously at any boy who tried to take them.

'Oh, come on,' said Jem finally, mopping the blood off his cuts, 'We're just wastin' time.'

And he and Ned set off for Walworth.

19

'You can't cross the river 'less you got the ready. It's a ha'penny each,' said the tollman at Waterloo Bridge. 'And don't try and push through the hatch neither, or I'll call a bobby and have you arrested.'

'All right, don't get snaggy, we got the money,' said Jem, holding up the penny he'd stolen from Kate.

The bridge was a seething mass of people and vehicles, from heavy, lumbering wagons loaded down with hay and manure, their iron-rimmed wheels grinding and screeching over the cobblestones, to the jingling costermongers' carts pulled by consumptive little donkeys.

Horses slipped and fell on the wet stones, and drivers fought, lashing each other with their whips when their wheels interlocked. Several times the boys were jostled so hard they almost fell under the horses' hoofs and Ned, swerving to avoid a growler driven by an irate cabby, barged into a woman balancing a huge basket of eggs on her head. The basket toppled and the next minute the ground was awash with a sea of orange yolks.

'You . . .!' The thunderous expression on the woman's face and the words she used to describe Ned – and what she would do to him once she laid hands on him – persuaded the boys to run as fast as they could.

Once over the bridge they clambered down the steep stone steps that led to the banks of the river. All London's sewage flowed straight into the Thames, making the water smell so foul that many people kept a handkerchief over their nose as they walked by.

'What're they doin'?' said Ned, pointing to the women and children wading, some of them waist deep in the cold, stinking mud along the shore. 'Why do they keep bendin' over? They lookin' for some-thin'?'

'Course they are. They're mudlarks.'

'Doesn't look like much of a lark to me,' Ned said, shivering. 'That kid over there's so cold she's turned blue.'

'She's lookin' for stuff to sell.'

'What kind of stuff?'

'Stuff that falls off the boats or,' Jem winked, 'gets

pushed off when nobody's lookin' . . . Oy!' he shouted at an old woman.

'What?' she straightened up, the filth from the river dripping off her ragged clothes.

'What you got there, in your basket, missus?'

'A bit of rope, a bit of wood, some nails, a few bones,' she said, holding her back and grimacing with pain. 'D'you want to buy some, my tulip?'

Jem shook his head.

'What about some coal?' She held up a rusty old bucket. 'Just one penny for the lot.'

'Nah, I got no money.'

'Then hook it!' she snapped, waving him away. 'And let me get on with my work.' And bending double again she began to grope in the mud.

'D'you reckon it's worth a try?' said Ned.

'What the mudlark? Don't be daft. Pa says they only make about threepence a day, if they're lucky, and they rip their feet on bits of glass and nails and get sores all over their legs from the freezin' water and . . .'

'Jem, look, look!' cried Ned, grabbing his arm.

'What?'

'Over there. The kid right up to his waist . . . It's Billy!'

'Nah . . .'

'It is, it is! It's his cap, the one that used to be mine. It's got a big rip in it . . .'

'You're right, it is him. Billy! Billy!'

The two boys ran across the shore, waving their arms and slipping and sliding in the wet mud.

'Billy! Billy!'

'Why doesn't he answer?'

'Cos he's got cloth ears, you know that . . . Billy!'

'Lor', I can't wait to see Ma's face when we get him home.'

'Billy, what's wrong with you, you little . . . Oh!' Jem skidded to a halt as the small boy turned and stared at him.

'I ain't Billy,' he muttered, reaching down into the water again. 'My name's Albert.'

Jem's face fell and Ned swallowed hard.

'I could've sworn . . .'

'Yeh, me too.'

' It looked just like him . . .'

'Come on, let's go.'

And hunching their shoulders against the biting wind they trudged back across the shore with hearts as heavy as the leaden skies above them.

20

'Why, my dear, what's wrong?' said Mrs Bullock anxiously. 'You're not eatin' your breakfast. I'm sure the eggs are fresh, I only got them from the market yesterday. And the bacon . . .' she picked up a piece and sniffed it, 'smells all right.'

'There's nothin' wrong with the grub, Flo,' growled her husband. 'It's him.' He jabbed his knife at Billy, who was cowering in a corner. 'I gone and lost my appetite on account of him. Made a right mess of the job at the Earl o' Clarendon's, he did. A right mess.'

'I'm not surprised, my dear. Soon as I clapped eyes on him I thought that one's a duffer, he won't bring us nothin' but grief. If I was you I'd sell him to One-eyed Eric in Bermondsey. He'll give you a tanner for him.'

Clem, who had been sitting at the table sewing, drew in her breath sharply. 'Nah, Dad, don't do that,' she said, hobbling over to Billy and putting her arms around him. 'He's too little to be a tosher.'

'What's a tosher?' Billy whispered in her ear.

'Someone what looks for stuff in the sewers. They manage pretty tidy cos they find all kinds of things down there — bits of iron and copper and sometimes coins, if they're lucky, and bits of silver and jewellery. But it's a killin' dodge. Most of them get sucked down into the mud and drowned or they lose their way in all them twists ands turns and never come out again or the rats rip them to pieces or the roof falls in on them and buries them alive or they choke to death cos of the fumes or . . .'

With a scream of terror Billy dived under the table.

'It'd polish him off, Dad,' said Clem.

'All right, my lovely. But I'm not sendin' him up no more chimneys neither, cos he hasn't got the brains to find his way down again,' said the sweep-master scornfully.

'But he could help us with the other jobs, Mr B,' said Pete. 'We got a big one tonight.'

'Doin' what?'

'He might make a good canary.'

'Nah, he's not strong enough.'

'What about a crow then? Billy, come here,' said

Pete. And reaching under the table he grabbed the little boy by the collar and yanked him out. 'You ever been a crow?'

'Nah, I always been a boy, long as I remember, but I could try bein' a crow,' said Billy, who was anxious to please the irate sweepmaster. Though,' his face fell, ' I don't think I'd be much good at flyin' cos I haven't got no wings.'

'Oh, blow me tight!' muttered Mr Bullock, laughing despite himself. 'The block'ead doesn't even know what a crow is.'

'A crow isn't a bird, Billy,' Pete explained to him, 'leastways, not the kind we're talkin' about. A crow's the person that stands outside a house while the rest of us are inside nickin' stuff. Then if anyone comes along, like a crusher, the crow gives us a warnin' signal so we can cut and run.'

'And a canary's the one that carries the swag away afterwards, so we don't get caught red-handed with it,' explained Dick.

'Only we don't want another canary cos Harry does a very nice job for us. But we do need a crow,' said Mr Bullock. 'I don't know about him though,' he glared at Billy, 'straight I don't.'

'Give him a chance, Mr B,' pleaded Pete.

'Yeh, go on, Dad,' said Clem. 'Let him have a go.'

'You got to keep a sharp lookout the whole time we're in the house,' warned Mr Bullock, 'and give us a whistle the minute you see anythin' suspicious. You can whistle, can you?'

Billy nodded.

'Well go on, then, let's hear you.'

The boy puckered his lips and blew till his front teeth rattled. But no sound came out.

'Try it like this,' suggested Dick, putting his fingers in his mouth and giving a shrill whistle.

But Billy had no luck with his fingers, although he did succeed in sucking off a lot of the soot.

'A animal noise is a good signal for a crow,' said Harry. 'Let's hear you bark like a dog, Billy.'

'Woof woof.'

'Nah, that wouldn't fool anyone. What about a cat?'

'Miaow.'

'What about a bird?'

'Oh, give over,' snapped the sweepmaster. 'You know he's only goin' to say, "Tweet tweet". He can't do nothin' proper.'

'But he'll be all right if someone learns him, Dad,' said Clem.

'And we got to have a crow, Mr B,' said Pete. 'We don't want to do the job tonight without one, do we?'

'Nah, there isn't time to learn him nothin'.'

'I can learn him to sound just like a tomcat,' said Clem.

'Nah, he'll never . . .'

'Let me try, Dad. Please.'

The sweepmaster looked into his daughter's imploring eyes. 'All right,' he nodded. 'You got a soft heart, my darlin'. But I tell you this,' he turned to Billy, 'one mistake and I'll sell you to One-eyed Eric . . . Nah, better still,' he snarled as tears began to flow down the little boy's cheeks, 'I'll let the Terror have you, then you'll really have somethin' to grizzle about.'

21

'Can't you go a bit faster?' Jem grumbled as they weaved their way through the busy backstreets that ran parallel to the river.

'We been walkin' for miles and miles. I'm wearin' my feet out,' moaned Ned. 'Anyway, I don't think you know where you're goin'.'

'I do.'

'Oh yeh? Are we near Walworth, missus?' Ned called to an old woman selling flowers.

'Bless you, no, my ducky, you're goin' the wrong way for Walworth. It's back there,' she said, pointing.

'We just come from there,' grumbled Ned. 'You said . . .' he rounded angrily on Jem.

'It wasn't me, it was Cousin Annie. She said go over Waterloo Bridge and turn left.'

'Where you come from, my tulips?' said the flower seller.

'Devil's Acre.'

'Devil's Acre? Lor, you wasted a lot of time and

shoe-leather. You should have gone over *Westminster* Bridge and then straight on.'

'When I get back I'm goin' to murder Cousin Annie,' fumed Jem.

'You mean *if* you get back,' said Ned darkly.

'If I was you I'd get a omnibus,' said the flower seller. 'Takes you right to Walworth, it do. Not that I've ever been there. I never go to them foreign parts if I can help it. The people don't seem the same as us.'

'So now what'll we do?' Ned fumed. 'You got to pay to go on a omnibus and we haven't got a farthin' between us.'

'Is your finger still bleedin'?'

'Nah, it's stopped.'

'Let's see.'

Ned showed him the deep gash the rat had made. The blood had thickened and was beginning to form a scab, but Jem squeezed it so hard the wound opened and blood spouted from it again.

'Ouch!' Ned sprang back. 'That does it,' he snarled, his face contorted with rage. 'I've had about enough of you.' And he raised his fists.

'S'cuse me, Your Honour,' said Jem, ignoring Ned and going up to a cherubic-faced old man. 'Could you help us? My brother's just had his finger bitten by a snake. Show the gen'leman, Ned.' And he grabbed his brother's bloody finger and held it up for the man to see.

'A snake?' the man exclaimed in disbelief.

'Yeh, it came out of the drains over there, enormous it was, about as big as . . .' Jem stretched his arms wide. 'It bit my brother and . . .'

'It *bit* him?'

'Yeh, bit him real hard, didn't it, Ned?'

Ned kept his mouth resolutely shut and stared at the ground. He wouldn't go along with Jem's dodge but he wouldn't spoil it either, for they needed the money for the omnibus.

'But snakes don't have teeth,' said the man, looking perplexed.

'They do in Australie, Your Worship. Big teeth they got there, like carvin' knives.'

'But how did a snake get here from Australia?'

'It must've hid itself in one of them boats,' said Jem, pointing vaguely in the direction of the river. 'Anyway,' he hurried on before the old man could ask any more awkward questions, 'it sunk its teeth in Ned's finger and wouldn't let go. Terrible struggle I had gettin' it off. Now I got to get him to a hospital before he drops dead cos he's losin' a lot of blood, aren't you, Ned?' he said, squeezing his brother's finger so hard that Ned cried out in pain. 'But we haven't got the needful for the omnibus.'

'Dear me, I'd take you there myself but I have an appointment at nine. Here,' the old man dipped into his pocket and, pulling out a money purse, pressed a shilling into Ned's hand.

'Now go straight to the hospital,' he said. 'And good luck to you, you poor fellow . . . Are you quite, quite sure it was a snake that bit him?' he frowned at Jem.

'Sure as my name's John Smith, Your Highness,' said Jem, putting his hand over his heart.

'And where is it now?'

'Went back down the drain.'

'The best place for it,' muttered the man, hurrying away.

'Jammy!' exclaimed Jem, grabbing the shilling. 'We got the fare for the omnibus. We're goin' to Walworth in style, we are. And,' he drew a silk handkerchief from his pocket, 'you can wrap this round your finger to stop it from bleedin'.'

'Well, I'll be jiggered!' exclaimed Ned. 'I never saw you take that off him.'

'Course you didn't,' said Jem, swelling with pride. 'I'm a professional, I am.'

22

The Mateys' housebreaking job that night was to be at the home of Joseph Bickerstaff, a wealthy lawyer who lived in Holborn.

'It's end of terrace, in a very quiet neighbourhood. Mostly decent-livin', respectable people who mind their own business, aren't they, Pete?' said Mr Bullock, for he and Pete had swept the chimneys there many times and knew the layout of the house like the back of their soot-covered hands. 'Bickerstaff's a bachelor, so there's no missus and brats to worry about, none that he'd own up to leastways, and the crusher on the beat in that part of the world is Spooner. He's an old bloke, they call him Dot and Carry One on account of his bad leg, which slows him up a treat. He won't give us no trouble.'

'Sounds jammy,' grinned Dick.

'Dead easy,' said Harry, nodding.

'Old Bickerstaff has his supper and goes out straight after in a silk top hat and a black cloak lined with red satin – dressed up to the knocker, he is,' said Pete. 'He don't get back for hours 'n hours, so we got plenty of time to do the job and scarper.'

'What about his housekeeper? Still Mrs Osborne, is it?'

'It is, Mr B.'

'Pity. She's a nosy old judy, always peerin' round the curtains to see what everyone else is doin'.'

'Yeh, but the last time we were there she said she'd got the rheumatics comin' on real nasty, so she spends most of the time in the kitchen while the maids run about doin' everythin'. Anyway, I don't reckon she'll be lookin' round curtains, not at that time of night,' Pete reassured him.

'Righto.' The sweepmaster nodded. 'Now here's the plan. You and Dick and me'll do the job. We'll get in through the kitchen door and go up to the first floor. The stuff we're after's in his study.'

'What is it, Mr B?'

'Goblets.'

The Mateys looked at each other, perplexed.

'Goblins?' said Dick.

'Goblets, you fat'ead – cups, splendiferous cups. Gold and silver. Some with jewels stuck in them.'

'Crikey!'

'Worth a fortune they are. Old Bickerstaff collects

 151

them. Course, they're all in a cabinet that's locked, but that won't give us no trouble.' The sweepmaster grinned. 'I'd like to see the lock I can't pick.'

'What about me, Mr B?' said Harry.

'You'll wait round the corner out of sight with the cart same as usual, ready to drive up when Billy gives the signal the job's done and we're ready to leave.'

To familiarize Billy with the scene of the crime, that afternoon Pete took him to the street where the lawyer lived and the two of them played hopscotch on the corner.

'You see anythin' that's likely to give us a problem, like old Bickerstaff comin' back early or a suspicious lookin' cove hangin' around, you know what to do, don't you, Billy?' said Pete. 'One miaow warns us somethin's up. Two miaows tells Harry to bring the cart round, so's we can get away sharp like.'

Billy nodded. 'I'm gettin' real good at miaowin'. Listen . . .'

'Cut it!' hissed Pete, slapping a hand over Billy's mouth. 'You'll give the game away.'

23

Jem and Ned had a spot of bother getting on the bus to Walworth, although they showed their shilling to the conductor, which was more than enough to take the two of them there.

'Filthy ragamuffins,' muttered some of the passengers.

'Guttersnipes.'

'Crawling with vermin, no doubt.'

'Don't let them on.'

'I can't stop them, missus, if they've got the money to pay their fares,' said the conductor in something of a quandary. 'It's a rule of the company that anyone who can pay the fare can get on for a ride – long as they behave themselves, of course.'

'Then send them outside, for goodness' sake, as far from decent folk as possible.'

'Go on then, up with you,' said the conductor, relieved that the problem had been solved to everyone's satisfaction.

'We wanted to go on top anyway,' retorted Jem, sticking his thumb to his nose.

'Yeh, we don't want to sit down here with you lot,' added Ned, 'cos we might get fleas.'

And they shinned up the iron ladder on the outside of the bus.

Since it was a bitterly cold day there was nobody on the top deck, so they had a choice of the seats which ran back to back down the middle. Of course, they chose the two at the front, right over the horses and next to the driver, a sturdy man in a white top hat, a rose in his buttonhole and a cigar clamped between his lips – a generous gift from one of his regular passengers.

'Here, guv,' Jem said, tapping him on the shoulder, 'could I have a go?'

'Don't you go disturbin' me, boy,' said the man sternly. 'If I don't keep to the timetable I'll be charged a fine, even if I'm only a minute late. So you just sit down and be quiet.'

And with a, 'Gee up there!' he urged the horses on.

They trotted along at a sedate pace while Jem and Ned, unable to contain their excitement at being on a bus for the first time, jumped up and down on the seats and leaned over the rail yelling rude remarks at people in the street below until the conductor came

up and told them that if they didn't stop misbehaving he'd turn them off . . . 'And you won't get your money back neither.'

'Can't we go no faster, guv?' Jem asked the driver.

'No, we can't. If I let my horses gallop, and somebody reported me to the guv'nor, I'd lose my job – and I can't afford that, not with a wife and ten children to look after.'

'I reckon we're never goin' to get to Walworth at this rate,' Jem whispered to his brother. 'Go on, Ned, give them horses a bit of encouragement with your catapult.'

'Nah, I don't think I should,' Ned frowned.

'Why not?'

'Cos it's dangerous. They might bolt.'

'Look, we got to get to Walworth, find Billy and get back home before dark and we're never goin' to do it if them horses don't move a bit faster. I'm not sayin' you should make them go mad, just give them a bit of encouragement. There's nothin' criminal about that, is there? They can't put us in clink just for aimin' a pebble at a horse's bum.'

'But . . .'

'Oh drat!' Jem growled. 'Now we're slowin' down'. Guv,' he tapped the driver on the shoulder again, 'why we stoppin'?'

'To let people on and off, of course. Daft question,' he grumbled.

'How long we got to wait then?'

'Till the people what wants to get off get off and them that wants to get on get on.'

'Come on, come on, look sharp there!' Jem shouted at the passengers, leaning over the side of the bus. 'Oy, you . . . Yeh, you, the devil-dodger,' he yelled at an elderly man who was chatting with a friend. 'You gettin' on or not? We can't hang about all day waitin' for clack-boxes.'

'Impudent rascal!' shouted the clergyman, waving his walking stick at him.

'I'm not warnin' you again,' said the conductor, clambering up the back of the bus. 'If you don't behave . . .'

'All right, all right,' Jem sat down. But as soon as the conductor had gone he was on his feet again, pestering the driver.

'We goin' to stop again before we get to Walworth, guv.'

'Course we are.'

'How many times?'

'Whenever people want to get on and off.' And at that very moment a woman stepped into the road, waving her umbrella at the driver, who pulled his horses to a halt.

Jem's face puckered into a worried frown. 'Crikey, we won't get there till Christmas at this rate,' he whispered to his brother. 'Billy'll be . . . I mean, he might be . . . gone.'

'Yeh, you're right,' said Ned gravely. And taking his catapult out of his pocket he loaded it with one of the small, sharp stones he always kept for just such an emergency.

'Aim for the horse on the right,' suggested Jem. 'She looks more sprightly.'

Ned held up the catapult, pulled back the elastic and fired. The first pebble missed the mare by a yard and pinged off the top hat of a man on the pavement. The second landed in a baby's perambulator and the third hit a tramp on the nose.

'Oh, give over, you'll hit everyone in London before you get anywhere near that horse,' cried Jem, wrenching the catapult from Ned's hand. And pushing him aside he leaned over the front rail, took careful aim at the mare's shining rump and fired.

The startled animal reared up, ears flat, eyes staring, and took off at a gallop, the other horse, omnibus and passengers careering along with it, whether they wanted to or not.

The driver, taken by surprise, heaved on the reins and yelled at his team to stop, but Jem leaned over his shoulder and yelled even louder so that the poor horses received a confusing torrent of, 'Whoa there! Whoa!' 'Gee up! Gee up!' 'Whoa, I say! Whoa!'

This, combined with the shrieks of 'Help! Help!' from the passengers on the lower deck, only encouraged the horses to go faster and they galloped madly through the narrow streets, the bus swaying behind them, overturning stalls and sending pedestrians flying for their lives.

'There goes another one!' cried Jem, as a fellow pushing a barrow of potatoes disappeared in the gutter under the full weight of his load. 'It's worth sixpence, this is!' he shouted, as a costermonger's stall collapsed, spewing fruit and vegetables all over the road.

The joyride was brought to an abrupt halt, however, by two policemen who, seeing the runaway bus careering towards them, leaped at the lead horse's head most courageously and hung on, forcing the animal to stop.

'Thank goodness. Oh, thank you, thank you, constables,' cried several of the elderly ladies on the lower deck – at least those who hadn't fainted or had a heart attack.

Once the horses were calmed and tethered the

two policemen approached the driver, who was still in a state of shock.

'What happened? What startled them?' they asked him.

When the poor fellow could speak, he pointed to the top deck with his whip and gasped, 'Those boys.'

'Let's get off,' Ned whispered urgently in his brother's ear. 'If we don't move plaguy quick we'll be up before the magistrate again.'

They hurtled down the ladder and barged through the large crowd that had gathered around the bus in the hope of seeing a dead body or two.

'There they are, constable!' cried one of the passengers, waving her umbrella at Jem and Ned. 'There are your villains!'

'Stop them!' shouted the policemen. 'Stop those boys!'

Hands reached out to grab them, but Jem and Ned were too fast. Away they went, running like the wind down side streets and alleyways, the policemen in hot pursuit. But the men were exhausted after their tussle with the horses and they soon gave up.

'It's all right,' said Jem, leaning against a lamp-post to get his breath back. 'We lost them.'

'Yeh, and we lost ourselves too,' snapped Ned, doubled up from the pain of his stitch. 'Again.'

'Stop glumpin',' snapped Jem, as Ned hunched his shoulders and turned away sullenly. 'We're not lost ... We in Walworth, guv?' he called out to a man selling cockles and whelks from a cart.

'You are indeed.'

'Where's the George'n Dragon?'

'Go to the end of this road, past the brewery, down 'Angman's Lane, take a third right and you'll see it straight ahead.'

Ten minutes later the boys were back.

'I told you,' said the cockle and whelk seller irritably, 'go to the end of this road, past the brewery, down 'Angman's lane, take a third right ...'

'Yeh, yeh, all right,' said Jem. And they started out again.

'We went wrong here last time,' said Ned when they got to the end of Hangman's Lane. 'That bloke said take a third right and you'll see it straight ahead. But we took a third left and ...'

'He *said* third left.'

'He did not.'

'He did ... Oy, missus!' Ned shouted at a woman down on her hands and knees scrubbing her doorstep, 'd'you know where the George'n Dragon is?'

'Don't be soft, son,' she said, 'everybody knows

where it is. Go back down here to the main road and it's starin' you in the face.'

'Is that where the Terror hangs out?'

The woman frowned. 'What d'you want to know that for?'

'Cos we want to see him.'

'See the Terror? You must be loonies,' she muttered. And shooting the boys a fearful glance, she picked up her bucket and hurried into her house, slamming the door shut.

24

The George and Dragon was a large, busy pub with wrought-iron gas lamps hanging over the entrance and windows and mirrors of frosted glass with elaborate designs carved into them. Although it was early in the evening the bar was already full of a noisy crowd of men and women drinking tankards of ale and porter, none of whom paid any attention to Jem and Ned except the landlord.

'I don't want no dirty sweeps in here,' he said, grabbing them by the ears and pushing them out into the street. 'You use that entrance in the future,' he pointed to a side door, 'and don't let me see you in the saloon again or I'll tell the Terror.'

And he went back into the pub, wiping his hands on his apron.

'Right, so now we know we come to the right place for the Terror,' said Jem, and he rapped on the side door with his knuckles.

An elderly woman, her head and shoulders

buried in a tattered scarf to protect her from the cruel wind, muttered something to Ned as she walked past.

'What'd she say?' asked Jem.

'She said, "I'd stay well clear of that place if I was you."'

'Sappy old trout,' scoffed Jem. But Ned grabbed his hand before he could knock on the door again.

'Jem, she's right. This bloke's dangerous. We could get ourselves killed.'

'Get off!' Jem shook himself free of Ned's grip. 'I didn't come all this way for nothin'.'

'But what if Billy isn't here?'

'Then we'll soon find out, won't we?'

'But if we don't get back soon, Pa'll . . .'

'Look, go home if you want to. But I'm stayin.'

'So am I.'

'Right,' said Jem. And he pounded the door with the flat of his hand.

After a minute or two a shrill voice grumbled, 'All right, all right, I'm comin'. No need to break the bleedin' door down. Who is it, anyway?'

'It's me and Ned.'

'Who's me?'

'Jem.'

'Jem who?'

'Perkinski.'

Heavy bolts were drawn back, and a woman poked her head round the door, her hair piled high in a mass of dirty waves and curls, her face heavily painted with rouge and mascara.

'Did you say Perkins*ki*?' she asked, the corners of her mouth beginning to turn up in a sneering smile.

'Yeh.'

At that she burst into such a torrent of giggles that the tears streamed down her cheeks in black rivulets. 'Pleased to meet you, I'm sure, Mr Perkins*ki*. My name's Nell. Nell Smith*ski*.' This sent her off into shrieks of laughter again.

'Look,' snapped Jem, 'we didn't come all this way just to see you bustin' your sides about our name. We want to see the Terror.'

Immediately the woman stopped laughing. 'He doesn't live here,' she said, giving him a cold, hard look.

'We were told he did.'

'Well, he's not in.'

'Pity, cos we got some rats for him.'

'Rats? I don't see no rats. Where've you got them – under your hat?' And she snatched Jem's wide-awake off his head and shook it.

'We got sacks and sacks of them,' he said, grabbing

it back and replacing it on his head with an air of injured dignity, 'country rats they are, best we could find. Fat as cats, real heavy. That's why we couldn't bring them. But we will if the Terror's interested in buyin' them.'

The woman hesitated, narrowing her eyes suspiciously.

'All right,' she said, opening the door wide enough for them to squeeze through, 'wait here. And don't move till I tell you,' she added, running up a flight of narrow stairs.

The boys waited in a dingy passageway, which smelt stale and musty.

'I don't like this place.' Ned shivered. 'It's got a creepy feel to it.'

'Nah, it hasn't,' said Jem, pulling his sleeves down hastily so that his brother couldn't see the gooseflesh that covered his arms.

'It has,' insisted Ned. 'It's like a graveyard. It's . . .'

'Stop that clackin' and get up here, quick about it,' the woman shouted from the top of the stairs. 'And listen,' she whispered urgently when they reached the landing, 'don't say nothin' about the Terror's . . .' She tapped her nose. 'Don't even look at it.'

'Why?' said Ned. 'What's wrong with his . . .?'

'You goin' to keep me waitin' much longer?' rasped a voice.

'Sorry, Terror, sorry, they're comin',' said Nell nervously. And she pushed Jem and Ned ahead of her into a small room.

The only light came from an oil lamp on a table in the corner and a dull fire glowing in the grate. On either side of the fire sat two men. One was old, his body shrunken, his face weathered and wrinkled. Wisps of white hair covered his cheeks and stuck out from under his battered hat. In his lap nestled a large grey rat, which he stroked lovingly. Another sat on his shoulder and, as the boys watched in horror, two more appeared from under his jacket. The old man grinned at them, revealing teeth as sharp and yellow as the rats'.

The other man sat with his back towards them, gazing into the fire.

'Terror, this is Jem and Ned Perkin*ski*,' said Nell. And she went off into peals of laughter. But the man threw up his hand in an impatient gesture and she immediately fell silent, gnawing at her lip as if she were trying to bite back the words that had displeased him.

The boys waited, Jem staring at the man's back, Ned looking nervously around the room, peering

into the shadows. Jem opened his mouth to say something, but Nell nudged him and shook her head. Only the ticking of the clock on the mantelpiece and the occasional rustling of the coals as they settled in the grate disturbed the ominous silence.

At last, like an actor waiting in the wings, sure of himself, sure of his audience, the Terror turned very slowly towards them, revealing his face inch by inch.

Ned let out a little cry and backed towards the door, scrabbling for the handle, but Jem stood his ground, trying hard not to flinch or show the fear and revulsion he felt. Steadily he gazed at the man's deeply scarred and pitted skin, the thin lips twisted to one side in a permanent grimace, the pale eyes devoid of all feeling, the two red-rimmed holes that were all that was left of his nose.

'Well?' said the man, and his voice came out as a snuffling, whistling sound that sent fear shimmering up and down Jem's spine. 'Where are all them rats then?'

'We . . . we haven't got them with us, guv,' said Jem. 'We just come to . . . er, to . . . er . . .' he stammered, losing his nerve as the Terror's eyes bore into his like shards of glass. 'We just come to . . .'

'But we'll go if you like,' said Ned, flattening

himself against the door so hard he seemed to be pushing his body through it.

'Oh, I see,' jeered the Terror, and his deformed mouth twisted into a grotesque parody of a smile. 'So this is just a social call, is it? You just popped in to enquire about my health, did you?'

He looked at Nell and the old man and they laughed obediently.

'I tell you what.' The Terror leaned towards the boys, lowering his voice to a menacing whisper, 'I think you're up to no good, you two. I smell a rat,' he said, tapping the two gaping holes beneath his eyes.

Ned, thinking it was meant to be a joke, let out a high-pitched squeal of hysterical laughter. Too late he realized his mistake. The Terror sprang out of his chair, his eyes glittering, and grabbed him by the shoulders, digging his fingers into the boy's flesh.

'Think it's funny, do you?' he rasped. 'Think I'm a clown, do you?'

Ned opened his mouth but no words came out.

'I don't like people laughin' at me. Don't you never laugh at me again. Now, you tell me the truth. Why are you here, eh? Pigs' narks, are you? Crushers sent you to spy on me, did they? Come on, spit it out or I'll choke it out of you!'

'We . . . we haven't come to spy on you, guv.

Honest. We . . . we came here to get Billy,' babbled Ned before Jem could stop him.

'Billy?' The Terror thrust his face closer to Ned's. 'What're you talkin' about. Who's Billy?'

'My b . . . brother.'

'Never heard of no Billy. You're makin' it up, aren't you? You're a liar!' snarled the Terror. 'But I'll make you talk.' And he put his hands on Ned's windpipe and pressed hard.

Ned let out a spluttering, gurgling sound as he gasped for air and his head fell forward limply.

'Here, you leave him alone!' cried Jem. And he sprang at the man, fists flying.

With a bellow of rage the Terror grabbed him by the collar and slammed him and Ned against the wall so hard all the breath was knocked out of their bodies.

'You'll be sorry you tried to make a fool of me!' he roared, his face contorted with rage. 'You'll wish you'd never been born by the time I'm finished with you!'

25

The night of the burglary was damp and misty.

'Stunnin!' said Mr Bullock, his dour face breaking into a rare smile. 'Nobody'll be about in this kind of weather, so the streets'll be nice and quiet.'

'But what if Bickerstaff doesn't go out neither?' said Dick anxiously.

'Nah, he'll go out, all right' said Pete. 'Nothin' keeps him home, not even a pea-souper. Fancies himself a man about town does old Bickerstaff,' he sniggered. 'He's a real ladies' man.'

Mr Bullock was doubly pleased when they arrived at Holborn to discover that one of the gaslights near the house had failed, so that their end of the street was plunged into darkness.

'Luck's on our side for a change,' he said, parking the horse and cart around the corner, away from suspicious eyes.

Pete, who had been sent on ahead, reported that all had gone according to plan.

'Bickerstaff left after supper, as per usual, and Mrs Osborne and the maids have gone to bed. I saw them go up to their rooms in the attic and the candles were snuffed out a while back. Old Dot and Carry One's on the beat, but his lumbago must be playin' him up a treat, cos he's limpin' more than usual. If you ask me,' he said sniffily, 'he's too ancient for the job. He couldn't catch a snail on crutches.'

'Well, I reckon this is goin' to go right as ninepence,' said Mr Bullock, 'provided nobody makes a pig's breakfast of it,' he added, staring pointedly at Billy.

'Don't vex yourself, Mr B, Billy'll be all right. He knows what he's got to do, don't you, nipper?' said Pete.

'Yeh. I'm goin' to hide behind the railin's and if I see somethin' wrong, like Mr Bigglestuff comin' back early, I give one loud miaow and . . .'

'Nah, nah, not loud, you stupe. Just a nice, normal miaow.'

'I give a nice, normal miaow,' Billy corrected himself. 'And when we're ready to push off, I give two loud . . . I mean two nice, normal miaows.'

'And you'd better get it right,' said the sweepmaster, 'cos if we get collared and pulled up before the magistrate it'll be the gallows for me and hard labour for you lot.'

The Mateys settled down to wait in the cart until every light in every house on the street had been extinguished and all the residents were tucked up in their beds. Billy, Dick and Harry slept soundly under the sooty sacks, but Mr Bullock was too nervous to relax. He lit his pipe and walked up and down, stopping every now and then to calm the horse, which tossed its head and stamped impatiently.

Pete, who had been keeping a lookout, returned just before midnight to say that the time was right to get going.

'Good,' Mr Bullock nodded. 'Here comes Dot and Carry One now, still limpin',' he noted with satisfaction as the policeman came round the corner.

The sweepmaster took out his fob watch and waited for the man to disappear round the other corner.

'Right!' he said. 'We got exactly ten minutes before old peg leg comes back. Let's get goin', lads.' And the four of them stole down the street to the lawyer's house, leaving Harry in charge of the cart.

With a glance to left and right to make sure they weren't observed, Mr Bullock, Dick and Pete ran down the area steps to the basement while Billy squatted behind the railings.

At the kitchen door Mr Bullock worked quickly. Opening the tool bag, Pete handed him the equipment he needed without being asked: a square piece of wood with a handle, which Mr Bullock placed over the pane of glass nearest the door handle, and a star glazer – a sharp knife, which he used to cut round the square and remove the glass. Then, putting his hand through the hole, he drew back the bolts and opened the door. Within seconds he and the Mateys were inside the house.

Billy stuck his head through the railings and looked up and down the street. Nothing stirred. It occurred to him this might be a good moment to escape. But in the next instant he abandoned the idea. Where was Devil's Acre? In which direction would he run? And, more to the point, Mr Bullock would be sure to catch up with him . . . He shuddered at the thought of the punishment the sweepmaster would dish out when he caught him.

'Pa . . .' he sighed. 'Ma . . .'

The thought of them brought tears to his eyes again but he hastily wiped them away in case anyone saw him.

To pass the time while he waited for Mr Bullock

and the Mateys to finish the job Billy hummed his way tunelessly through every song he knew, which was three, and repeated every swear word he'd ever heard, which was considerably more. But after a while he grew bored and began to fidget.

There was a moment's excitement when Spooner reappeared, grunting with every step. Billy shrank back into the shadows and held his breath. But when the policeman had gone boredom set in again.

Billy yawned.

Spooner plodded by a second time.

And a third.

Keep a sharp lookout all the time, Billy . . . Pete's warning rang in his ears.

'I must stay awake,' he told himself, yawning again. 'I must.' And leaning his head against the railings he closed his eyes and fell asleep.

26

Jem and Ned had been thrown into a cold, dark cellar beneath the George and Dragon, its walls slimy with mould, its ceiling festooned with cobwebs. Hundreds of black, oily sacks were piled in towering stacks on the floor and the stale air was heavy with the stench of soot.

'That bloke's mad,' whispered Ned, clutching his bruised neck. 'He's stark ravin'. And so were we for comin' here.'

'Don't start that again,' growled Jem. 'We came here to find Billy and—'

'And we never will. You heard what Gran said, the Terror snatches kids like him off the street and chucks them in the river.'

'Only when they grow too big to go up chimneys. But Billy's still little. He's just right for a sweep. Anyway, Gran said he's still alive.'

'Yeh, he was when she looked in that bit of glass. Don't mean he is now.'

'Crimes, Ned,' Jem exclaimed, 'you are such a misery guts.'

'I'm not. I just think we come on a wild goose chase.'

'Well, I'm goin' to find Billy, see if I don't! All I got to do is get out of here and . . .'

'Oh yeh? And how you goin' to do that? There's only one door and it's got about fifty bolts on it. Forget it, Jem, neither you nor me're never goin' to get out of here. We're done for. We're . . . Oh, Lor'!'

'What? What's wrong with you?'

'In that corner. I saw somethin' move.'

'Probably a rat or a spider.' Jem looked up at the gigantic cobwebs suspended like dirty lace from the ceiling. 'Look at that one,' he pointed. 'Big as a carter-wheel, it is. I reckon its legs are thicker than—'

'Hold your jaw, will you!' barked Ned, pulling up his collar. 'It wasn't no spider, anyway. There's somethin' under them sacks, somethin' big.'

'You'd best go see what it is then.'

'Me? Why me?'

'Cos you're the one that saw it.'

'Nah.' Ned backed away in alarm. 'Nah, I was . . . er . . . I was only kiddin' you. I was . . .'

'Whoa, you're right, there is somethin',' shouted

Jem, darting forward. 'I just seen it move. You get one side, Ned, and I'll get the other and we'll—'

'Nah, don't hurt me,' cried a small voice. 'Please.'

'Sounds like a nipper,' whispered Ned.

'Come on out,' said Jem.

'Don't hurt me,' pleaded the voice. 'I've not done nothin' wrong. Please don't . . .'

'Course we won't,' said Jem.

'Promise?'

'Yeh, promise. Come on out, so's we can see you proper.'

Very slowly the sacks parted and a small boy crawled out. He was not much older than Billy but his face was wasted away and his body stooped and shrivelled with weariness and starvation.

'Who're you?' demanded Jem.

The boy looked up at him fearfully, his eyes sunk deep in reddened sockets. 'Alfie,' he whispered.

'What you doin' here, Alfie?'

'I'm workin' for the Terror.'

'You a sweep?'

'I was. But I fell down a chimney and hurt myself real bad, so I couldn't do it no more, so now I work in the pub.'

'What, servin' booze?'

'Nah, I do all the cleanin'. I got to be up there real

early, cleanin' grates and lightin' fires and emptyin' slop buckets and fetchin' water and makin' beds and polishin' boots and scrubbin' floors and doin' the washin' and manglin' and ironin' and—'

'Blow me down,' exclaimed Ned, 'you must be dead beat after all that, a littl'un like you.'

The boy nodded. 'But I'm lucky cos I'm still alive. There've been loads of sweeps here, but when they got too big to go up chimneys the Terror . . .' He made a slashing movement as if he were chopping off someone's head.

'Blimey!' shuddered Ned.

'So how long you been here, Alfie?' said Jem.

'Don't know.' The boy shrugged. 'Ages'n ages. My dad sold cakes from his tray, and I'd walk alongside him shoutin', "Jam tarts! Coventries! Bowlas! Chonkeys! Jumbles!" Then one day when it was real hot my dad sent me to the pump to get him a drink of water, but I got lost on the way back. I kept runnin' up one street and down the other but I couldn't find him nowhere and then it got dark so I dossed down in a doorway and next mornin' a toff came along and he said he'd give me all the grub I wanted if I went home with him, and I was real hungry by then, so . . .' A tear stole out of his eye and wove its way slowly down his dirty cheek. 'I found out afterwards that the toff works for the Terror. He goes all over London lookin' for kids, promises them a nice warm bed and all the grub they can eat, then he brings them back,' he looked mournfully around the grim cellar, 'to this. Is that how he got you?'

'Nah,' said Jem. 'We come here of our own accord.'

Alfie stared at him in disbelief. 'Lor, you must be numbskulls gettin' mixed up with the Terror of your own accord,' he said. 'Anyone with half a brain would've run a mile in the other direction.'

It was as well that Jem had promised not to hurt the little boy because usually when somebody insulted him he had a tendency to flatten them. As it was he gulped hard and said, 'Yeh . . . well, we're lookin' for our brother Billy.'

'Billy?' Alfie shook his head. 'Don't know nobody called Billy. Why d'you think he's here?'

'Cos Gran said . . .' began Ned. But Jem cut him short. He had a feeling that telling Alfie their grandmother could call up spirits and read crystal balls might provoke more insults and keeping his fists away from the little boy's teeth would prove more difficult.

'Cos we found out Billy was a sweep, so we

reckoned he must be workin' for the Terror,' he said. 'But since he isn't here we'd best get goin'.'

'Goin'?' Alfie frowned. 'Goin' where?'

'To look for Billy, of course.'

'But you can't get out of here.'

'Course I can. I got out of worse places than this,' said Jem stoutly.

'Well, you'll never get out of here alive. You'd never get past Samson and Delilah for a start.'

'Who?'

'The Terror's dogs. Didn't you see them? Big as tigers, they are,' said Alfie, wide-eyed. 'They got teeth like this . . .' He held his fingers three inches apart. 'The Terror's trained them to be real vicious. They'd rip your leg off soon as look at you. I tried to escape once. Got as far as the corner, but Samson ran after me and . . .' He pulled up his sleeve and showed them a wicked scar that had puckered and withered the skin from his elbow to his shoulder. 'The Terror called him off but he said if I ever tried it again he'd let the dog kill me.'

Another tear followed the first down Alfie's cheek.

'Lor,' muttered Ned in dismay. 'We've come a mucker this time, Jem, and no mistake.'

'Shut it, knocker-face,' snapped Jem, 'we're not

dead yet. Who's the old fogey with the Terror,' he said to Alfie, 'the queer cove with rats runnin' all over him?'

'That's Jack Black. He used to be the Queen's rat-catcher.' The brothers sniggered. '*He did*,' Alfie protested. 'Now he looks after them for the Terror. They're in a cellar down here, hundreds of them,' he said with a shudder. 'Sometimes when Old Jack goes in to feed them you can hear them all squealin' fit to make your hair stand on end. I sometimes wonder what'd happen if they got out.'

'Stash it!' muttered Ned.

'You scared?' said Jem.

'Course I'm not.'

'Why're your teeth chatterin' then?'

'They're not. Anyway, it's cos I'm freezin'. It's plaguy cold in here.'

'Best way to keep warm is to croodle,' suggested Alfie. 'That's what me and my dad used to do. Dad wrapped himself round me and we kept warm as muffins.'

There was a lot of squabbling about who should sleep where, but it was finally agreed that since Alfie was the smallest he should sleep in the middle and they lay down, pressed their bodies close together and wrapped their arms around each other for warmth. But try as they might sleep would not come.

'I wish you'd stop scratchin',' complained Jem.

'It's the pesky fleas. I got a plague of them and they're bitin' me fit to bust,' said Ned. 'And I wish you'd stop coughin' and snortin' down my neck.'

'It's the soot. It gets up my nose. I can't hardly breathe. And stop wrigglin' about, Alfie,' Jem grumbled. 'That's twice you've stuck your elbow in my ribs.'

But despite the intense cold, the hardness of the floor, the spiders that skittered over their faces and the fleas, bugs and lice that bit them mercilessly, the three boys finally fell asleep, curled around each other like a nest of spoons.

27

Billy woke with a start. A sound had disturbed his slumbers. Yawning hugely he thrust his head through the railings and peered up and down the street in a sleepy kind of way. Then he stiffened. Two men and a boy were coming towards him, moving so furtively they looked decidedly suspicious.

'Don't give the warnin' signal unless you're dead sure somethin's up,' Pete had said.

So Billy waited.

When the three reached Mr Bickerstaff's house they stopped, conversing in whispers for a second. Then the men swarmed down the area steps while the boy took up his position in front of the railings, crouching low and looking up and down the street just as Billy had been doing.

Billy was furious. 'Oy!' he hissed, putting his foot through the railings and giving the boy such a kick on the backside he sent him sprawling across the pavement. 'Shove on one side, will you! You're blockin' my view.'

The boy gave a yelp as he landed on his hands and knees in the gutter.

'What's happenin'?' cried the two men in hoarse whispers, leaping back up the area steps in one bound. 'You all right, Fred?'

'There's someone in there.' The boy pointed to where Billy crouched in the shadows. 'He just gave me a wallop up the bum.'

A hand reached out and grabbed Billy.

'Pack off!' he yelled.

'Hold your jaw, you little varmint!' hissed the man, yanking him from his hiding place.

Realizing that his cover was blown Billy cried, 'Miaow!' to warn Mr Bullock and the Mateys.

'Stash it, I said!' The man clapped a hand over Billy's mouth. 'Shut up or I'll . . . Ayeeeeeee!' he screeched as Billy sank his teeth into the fleshy pad of his thumb.

'Miaow! Miaow! Miaow!' yodelled Billy, until it began to sound as if a dozen bloodthirsty tom cats were going at each other tooth and nail. 'Miaow! Miaow! Miaow!'

Lights sprang on in houses all down the street. Windows were thrown open. Angry faces appeared.

184

'This is too much!' cried an aggrieved voice. 'Somebody should put a stop to those wretched animals.'

'I'll get them, ma'am, don't you worry,' retorted an elderly man appearing in the window of the house opposite. And aiming a rifle he began firing wildly in all directions.

'See what you done now?' the man hissed in Billy's ear. 'Woke the whole street you have with that bloody racket.'

'Miaooow!' went Billy.

'What a caterwauling!' cried a shrill voice from the attic window in Mr Bickerstaff's house. 'This should shut them up.'

The next moment a bucket of icy water cascaded down on Billy's head.

'Blimey!' he cried, stunned.

'It can't be cats, Mrs Osborne,' said one of the maids.

'Course it is, girl.'

'Well, then, it's cats that talk cos one of them just said blimey.'

'Wash your mouth out with soap and water, Lucy,' scolded the housekeeper. 'Such disgusting language. I've never heard the like.'

The area door opened and Mr Bullock, Pete and

Dick came bounding up the steps at the same moment that Harry drove the horse and cart round the corner at the gallop.

There seemed to be some disagreement between the Mateys and the new set of burglars as to precisely whose patch it was and the two sides set about each other with fists and boots while Mrs Osborne and the maids tipped buckets of water over them, the neighbours shouted, the old gentleman fired his rifle at anything that moved, babies cried, dogs barked and Billy stared, open-mouthed.

Suddenly the cry went up, 'Crushers!', and as two policemen bore down on them spinning rattles the warring burglars took to their heels. Seeing that Mr Bullock and the Mateys were otherwise occupied Billy decided to seize his chance to escape and he too took off, running down the street at full pelt.

'There goes one of them!' voices shouted after him. 'Stop him! Stop thief!'

At the corner he turned briefly and looked back. To his relief he was not being followed. The policemen, who had come off the worse in their tussle with the burglars, were sprawled across the pavement, holding their heads and groaning. And of Mr Bullock and the Mateys there was no sight.

Billy was sad that he'd never see Pete and Dick

and Harry again. And he'd miss Clem. But as for her father . . .

'Good riddance!' he shouted. And made a very rude gesture.

28

Mr Bullock drove through the dark streets as if all the hounds of hell were after him. Time and again he shouted at Dolly, 'Gerrup, you lazy faggot! Faster! Go on, damn you, faster!' and brought his whip down hard on her rump.

The mare whinnied in fear and slithered and stumbled over the wet cobblestones, almost falling.

Pete watched with growing anxiety until he could stand it no longer. Taking his courage in both hands he said, 'Go easy on her, guv. She's old and a bit poorly.'

'I don't care if she's dyin',' yelled the sweepmaster, lashing her again. 'We got to get back quick or the crushers'll be after us.'

By the time he pulled up in front of the house Dolly was covered in sweat and foaming at the mouth. Leaping out of the cart Pete quickly unharnessed her and led her into a small, makeshift stable where he rubbed her down, covered her with a blanket and gave her a little water, talking to her softly all the time.

Mr Bullock pushed Dick and Harry into the house and bolted the door.

'What happened, my dear?' cried his wife, almost falling down the stairs in her alarm.

'What happened? What happened?' bellowed the sweepmaster, whose terror had turned to rage. 'I nearly got collared, that's what happened! Your husband nearly ended up on the gallows, that's what happened!'

Clem, who had followed her mother down the stairs, hobbled towards him, her face taut with fear. 'Oh, Dad, no!' she cried.

'It's all right, my princess. Don't you fret yourself,' he said, engulfing her in his arms and rocking her gently. 'Your old dad's come back to you. Your old dad's safe now.'

'But what hap—?' began his wife.

'Shh!' He put a finger to his lips and pointed at Clem, who had snuggled her head into the nape of his neck. 'I'll tell you later,' he whispered. 'We'd best go up to bed now. I'm fair done up. I'm—'

He was interrupted by a loud and urgent knocking at the door.

'It's them!' gasped Mrs Bullock, clutching her husband's arm. 'The crushers! They've come for you! They—'

'Nah, don't be daft, that's our secret signal.' He gave a nervous laugh. 'It's Pete. I must've locked him out.'

'Dad, where's Billy?' asked Clem as Pete came in, banging his feet and rubbing his hands together to get his blood circulating a little faster.

'I don't know and I don't care,' growled the sweepmaster.

'But—'

'Clem, if you love your old dad you'll never mention that little varmint's name in this house ever again. And that goes for you too,' he barked at the Mateys, who stood in a line gazing mutely at the floor. 'I ever hear you say Bi . . . that kid's name I'll tan your hide so hard you won't sit down for a week. That clear?'

The three boys nodded.

'Right, then. I'm off to bed.' And he mounted the stairs slowly, groaning a little at every step because the policemen had given him a few good whacks with their night sticks before he'd trounced them.

When the Bullocks had gone up to bed the Mateys curled up in front of the fire, snuggling as close to it as they dared. Dick and Harry cried out in their sleep as they relived the nightmare in Holborn, but Pete slept soundly until he was woken by someone tugging at his arm.

'What the . . .?' He sprang up.

'Shh!'

'Clem? What you doin' down here?' he whispered. 'If your dad . . .'

'He's fast asleep . . . Pete, where's "you know who"?'

'Don't know. We left him outside Old Bickerstaff's keepin' a lookout and some other cracksmen came along so he started miaowin'. Only 'stead of givin' two normal miaows to warn us, like you learned him, he started miaowin' like a looney tic. I reckon half of London must've heard him. I shouldn't be surprised if old Vicky didn't hear him in Buckin'am Palace. Course, the crushers came runnin' – I tell you, old Dot and Carry One can really move when he has to,' he said admiringly.

'But what about "you know who"?'

'Me and the Mateys and Mr B all legged it back to the cart, but he ran off in the other direction.'

'Poor little nipper,' Clem exclaimed, 'he'll get lost. He'll be so frightened.'

'Well, he's only himself to blame.'

'We got to find him, Pete.'

'*What?*'

'D'you know where his family lives?'

'Nah . . . Yeh, he said it was somewhere near the river.'

'Lor's sake,' huffed Clem, 'everybody in London lives somewhere near the river, you ninny.'

'Wait a crack, it's comin' back to me. He said he lives just by a church.'

'Oh well, that should be dead easy. There're only about a hundred churches in this town.'

'But it wasn't an ordinary church, Clem. It was a big'un, a real big'un. I got the name on the tip of my tongue . . . Somethin' Abbey.'

'St Paul's.'

'That's it . . . I think.'

'Righto, let's go.'

'Clem, you off your chump? Bil . . . I mean "you know who" could be anywhere. It'd be like lookin' for a needle in a . . .'

'But we got to try.

'Anyway, we couldn't walk that far.'

'We're not goin' to. We'll go in the cart.'

'But your dad . . .'

'It's Sunday, isn't it? He'll sleep all mornin', and by the time he gets up we'll be back.'

'But . . .'

'You don't have to come if you don't want to. I can drive the cart myself.'

'But you can't go alone. You're a girl.'

Too late Pete realized his mistake. Clem got to her feet and hobbled to the door in high dudgeon.

'Clem, wait!' Pete ran after her. 'I'll go with you.'

'Nah, you won't. You don't want to go with a *girl*,' she said in a voice heavy with scorn.

'I'm sorry, Clem. I just thought . . . Well, it's not easy for you . . . I mean . . .'

'You mean cos I got a club foot,' she rounded on him, hands on hips. 'You think I can't do nothin' just cos I'm a girl and a cripple.'

Pete blushed and hung his head.

'I can't say nothin' right, can I?' he mumbled. 'I got nothin' against girls, honest. My mum was one — well, when she was little — and she was the squarest moll you could ever meet. But I . . .' he hesitated, 'I don't want nobody to hurt you.'

Clem stared at him for a moment, unsure

whether to be angry that he felt she couldn't look after herself or pleased that he wanted to look after her. Then she touched his arm and said, 'Come on, let's go and find "you know who".'

29

Jem woke just before dawn.

The fog had lifted for once and a full moon rolled lazily across the clear sky like a giant snowball, its light piercing the soot-covered window of the sweeps' cellar and bathing everything in an eerie glow – the grimy walls and oily sacks and cobwebs thick as string. Ned was lying on his back fast asleep, his mouth wide open, but Alfie was sitting cross-legged on the floor, sobbing quietly.

Jem raised himself on his elbows, shivering, wondering where he was.

'Alfie?' he whispered, blinking and rubbing his eyes. 'What you cryin' about?'

'My dad.'

'What's wrong with your dad?'

'Nothin'.'

'Then why're you snivellin'?'

'Cos I won't never see him again.'

'Course you will. And your ma.'

'Nah, I won't. My mum died before I was born.'

'Well, what about your brothers and sisters.'

'I haven't got none.'

'Lor', we'd best get you back to your dad, then.'

'How?' Alfie turned to him, his tear-stained eyes full of hope.

'I'll think of somethin',' muttered Jem. 'Hey up, someone's comin'.'

'It'll be Nell with our grub,' whispered Alfie. 'Nell's worse than the Terror sometimes, 'specially when she's in a bad mood. Don't say nothin' to upset her. Nothin'.'

The boys heard the sound of bolts being drawn back, and the woman came in with a pitcher of water in one hand and a few scraps of stale bread in the other.

'Right, here you are, my little darlin's, here's your breakfast,' she said, throwing the bread on the filthy floor. 'Though why I should have to wait on you, I don't know. I'm not your bleedin' servant.'

Ned reached out eagerly but Nell kicked his hand away.

'It's not for you, Mr Perkin*ski*,' she snapped. 'It's for those that's worked for it. Anyway, you don't need nothin' to eat.' She grabbed Ned's arm and sank her long fingernails into his flesh. 'You got plenty of good meat on you, by the feel of it.'

Ned began to tremble violently.

'Cor, look at him, he's all of a quiver!' Nell roared with laughter. 'Scared, are you, my pet? Gettin' all hot and bothered? Here, this'll cool you down.' And she emptied the pitcher of ice-cold water over the boy's head.

'If you lot are thirsty,' she said, laughing fit to bust, 'the drinks are on him.'

'But I want some water,' whined Alfie.

'Shut up!' Nell's mood changed abruptly and she cuffed the boy so hard he fell, sprawling across the floor. 'And you two,' she beckoned to Jem and Ned, 'come with me. The Terror wants to see you.'

'Nah, we . . . we don't want . . . I mean we can't stop here cos we . . . cos we got to get home. Our ma and pa are waitin' for us,' stammered Jem.

Nell put her hands on her hips and stared at him in disbelief.

'*What – did – you – say?*'

Alfie squeezed his eyes tightly shut and covered his ears.

'He didn't say nothin',' Ned whispered. 'Did you?' he nudged his brother.

'Nah, nothin',' Jem muttered.

'I'm glad to hear it,' huffed Nell. 'Now come on!'

30

'Don't do nothin' to upset him, Jem,' whispered Ned as they scuttled up the narrow staircase with Nell cursing at their heels. 'Don't look at his . . .' He tapped his nose.

The Terror was sprawled in an armchair, a glass of gin and hot water on a table beside him, two large dogs of mixed breed chained to the leg of his chair. He had been drinking heavily, and his face in a drunken state was even more loathsome, the eyes colder, the deformed mouth stretched more tightly to one side, the gaping holes where his nose should have been more cavernous.

On the other side of the fire sat Old Jack, fast asleep, with two or three rats curled up contentedly in his lap.

'So? Have you come to your senses yet, young gen'lemen?' demanded the Terror as Nell pushed Jem and Ned into the room. 'Are you goin' to tell me why you're here? The truth, mind. I don't want no more cock'n bull stories or I'll set my dogs on you.'

Samson and Delilah stirred and growled.

'Not yet, my beauties,' rasped the Terror in a voice heavy with menace. 'Give these young gen'le-men the chance to explain themselves first . . . Well?' He leaned back in his chair and took a deep swig of gin. 'Go on, then. I'm listenin'.'

'It . . . It's my gran's fault, Your Honour,' said Jem. 'She told us that Billy was here.'

Jem had decided to tell the Terror the truth. Once the man knew they meant him no harm he would surely let them go.

'Your gran?' The Terror frowned. 'Do I know her?'

'Nah . . . Leastwise, I don't think so, Your Worship,' said Jem, putting his hands behind his back, so the Terror couldn't see them trembling. 'But she knows you. I mean she knows all about you . . .' he faltered, wondering if he'd gone too far.

The Terror leered at him. 'Knows all about me, does she? And what does she know, eh?'

Jem hesitated.

'I said, *What does she know*?' The Terror banged the arm of his chair, the noise increasing ominously as his patience decreased.

'Go on, for Lor's sake!' hissed Nell, jabbing Jem in

the ribs, for she knew that when the Terror flew into a rage it wouldn't just be the boys who were sworn at and beaten.

But Jem was in a quandary. He could hardly tell the Terror some of the dreadful things his grandmother had said about him.

Nell put her mouth close to his ear and whispered, 'He likes to hear how scared people are of him.'

'My gran says you're one of the wickedest men in London.' Jem spoke up, though he couldn't keep the fear out of his voice, try as he might.

The Terror frowned.

Jem looked at Nell, wondering what he'd done wrong.

'Not *one of the wickedest*, you little fool!' she hissed. 'There's nobody worse than the Terror.'

'I meant *the* wickedest man in London . . . in the whole of the world. Gran says you kill climbin' boys and chuck them in the river.'

'Oh I do, I do.' The Terror leaned forward and beckoned Jem towards him. 'And did your gran tell you that I . . .?' And winking at Nell, he mimicked slicing up a body with a knife and putting pieces in his mouth.

Jem bit his lip to stop himself from crying out,

but Ned shrieked and ran to the door, kicking it and tugging at the handle.

'What's wrong with him?' The Terror turned to Nell, feigning surprise.

'Anybody'd think you were goin' to eat him,' said Nell, joining in the game.

'Him? He's just a bag of bones. He wouldn't even make a decent bowl of soup,' chuckled the Terror. 'So your gran told you I'd got your brother, did she?' he said, turning to Jem. 'And what made her think that, pray?'

'Well, Your Nobleness, it's cos she sees things.'

'Spies on me, you mean?' The man sprang up, his face livid. 'I knew it! I knew you were pigs' narks. I knew—'

'Nah, nah, I mean she looked in her crystal and—'

'Her *what*?'

'It's a glass ball. She sees things in it. She saw Billy. And she saw you. Leastwise she said she did. But Pa said she was makin' it up. And he was right, cos Billy isn't here,' Jem babbled.

The Terror listened to him open-mouthed.

'A glass ball? Your gran sees things in a glass ball?' He sat down again, shaking his head in amazement. 'It's so ridiculous I believe you, straight I do. Nobody could make up a loony story like that. And what tickles me more,' he pointed a finger at the boys, 'is that I didn't have to steal you or buy you. I got you both for nothin' . . . Well, I got to thank your dear old gran for that.' And he slapped his thigh and guffawed, but there was no humour in his laughter and his eyes were as cold as steel.

Nell laughed too and kicked Old Jack on the shin so that he woke up and started to laugh, though he had no idea what he was laughing about.

'Tell you what I'm goin' to do,' the Terror said, silencing them with a glance, 'you young gen'lemen are no good as sweeps cos you're too big to get up chimneys, but since you're nice and strong I'm goin' to let you help Old Jack with his rats. Like rats, do you?'

'Yeh, I do,' Jem said.

'Ho, ho, we got a brave one here, Nell,' the man sneered. 'I wonder if he'll be so brave after he's been bitten by a dozen of them.' And he grabbed one of the rats in Old Jack's lap and hurled it at the boy.

Jem instinctively raised his hand to protect his face, and the frightened creature bit him and scampered into a corner, squeaking loudly.

'There! How did you like that, eh?' The Terror grinned.

'It's nothin',' said Jem defiantly, thrusting his bleeding hand into his pocket. 'I been bitten a lot harder than that.'

The smile froze on the man's lips.

'Don't hurt him, Terror,' Nell cut in quickly, putting herself between him and Jem. 'We got a big meetin' today and we could do with a bit of extra help.'

The Terror waved her aside and leaned back in his chair, scowling at the boys.

They waited, Jem trying to ignore the throbbing pain where the rat had sunk its teeth deep into his hand, Ned staring at the floor, the ceiling, the walls, anywhere but the man's hideously deformed face.

'All right,' he rasped, waving the boys closer to him. 'Now listen. You'll stay here long as you're useful, but if I hear you been blabbin' to anyone about me I'll . . .' He drew a dagger from the sleeve of his jacket and dug the point into Jem's throat so hard that blood trickled down his neck and stained his kerchief.

Jem flinched and cried out and the Terror smiled, pleased that he had forced the boy to show how frightened he was.

'And if you ever try to run away I'll come after you with my dogs,' he said, leaning back in his chair.

'I keep them nice and thin, nice and hungry . . . You get my meanin', do you?'

Samson and Delilah eyed the boys balefully.

'Yeh,' muttered Jem. 'We get your meanin', guv.'

31

Dolly was tired after her mad gallop home from the failed burglary, but Pete moved her along at a gentle pace, letting her find her own way over the slippery cobblestones and around the puddles. He had spread her blanket over the seat to protect Clem's clothes from the dirt and soot, and the girl huddled close to him as they made their way through the dark alleyways of the Rookery.

'You cold, Clem?' he asked.

She shook her head.

'You are. I can feel you shiverin'. Here, take this,' he said, pulling off his ragged jacket.

'Don't be soft,' she protested, trying to push him away. 'You'll freeze.'

'Course I won't,' he laughed, putting it round her shoulders. 'Matter of fact, I'm boilin',' he said, hastily wiping an icicle off the end of his nose.

By the time they reached High Holborn a watery sun was trying to light up the winter sky. On a weekday the street would have been teeming with people going about their business, but on a Sunday all was quiet. A few children were up and about, scouring the pavements for scraps of food dropped by the Saturday-night revellers or riffling through the pockets of men and women lying drunk in the gutter.

No cabs or buses clattered along the roads, no shops opened, no traders trundled their barrows through narrow lanes, shouting their wares. The devout went to church in the morning and evening and spent the rest of the day in sober meditation. Those of a less religious turn of mind slept late, ate as hearty a dinner as they could afford, put on their Sunday finery and went for a walk.

'Lawks, Pete, I do wish you'd stop yawnin',' grumbled Clem. 'You're settin' me off now.'

'I can't help it, Clem. I haven't had no sleep. I'm . . . Hey!' he cried in alarm as a brawny man with hard eyes and a jail-cropped head leaped on to the cart.

'Got somethin' for me, my ducky? Somethin' I could sell?' he said, fingering Clem's dress and jacket. 'Got a coin or two?' He reached into her pocket.

'Leave her alone!' shouted Pete, raising his whip.

'Not so fast, young'un,' growled the man, putting a knife to Clem's throat.

'Oy, Drake, can't you see that's Bullock's girl, you bleedin' idiot?' someone shouted at him. 'If he finds out you laid a finger on her he'll cut you to ribbons.'

'Oh sorry, sorry, my treasure,' said the man. And he jumped off the cart and slunk away.

'Did he hurt you?' said Pete, looking at her anxiously.

'Nah, I'm all right,' she said, pulling up the collar of his jacket so he couldn't see where the knife had pierced her flesh. 'Let's get goin'. Quick.'

Pete flicked the whip lightly on the mare's flanks, and she moved into a steady trot.

'Where does Bickerstaff live?' said Clem.

'Next road on the left. But I'm not going down it in case someone sees me.'

'Which way did Billy run?'

'Up that road and round the corner.' He pointed.

'Righto, let's go that way.'

'Clem . . .' Pete began in an exasperated voice.

'I know, I know, he won't be there. But we got to start somewhere, haven't we?'

'He's probably home by now.'

'Do you really think so?' said Clem, her eyes lighting up.

'Nah.' Pete shook his head. 'Knowin' him he's runnin' round and round in circles.'

As the sun rose higher more children began to appear on the streets, some in elegant clothes, chaperoned by equally well-dressed parents, others in rags, neither cared for nor wanted by anyone. Clem bent forward, looking eagerly into their faces. Several times she gave a little gasp and half rose in her seat, only to sink back again with a sigh.

'Is it far to St Paul's?' she said after a while.

'Miles and miles,' replied Pete disconsolately. 'I'm goin' to stop and give Dolly some oats.'

While he fed the mare, Clem closed her eyes and tried to pretend she was back in bed, snuggled under the big goose-feather eiderdown with her father on one side and her mother on the other. Sunday was her favourite day. Since nobody wanted their chimneys swept on the Sabbath, indeed any kind of work was frowned on, her father and the Mateys stayed home. While they played cards or fivestones before the fire, her mother cooked a leg of mutton and . . . The girl's reverie was interrupted by the sound of raucous laughter. Four or five young men were swaggering down the street, joshing each other in loud voices and occasionally glancing around to see who was admiring them in their flashy clothes.

'Look at them toffs, Pete,' Clem said.

'They're not toffs,' he said scornfully. 'Fancy themselves, they do. Try to pretend they're gentry. But they're no better than you'n me, Clem. Matter of fact they're a lot worse cos at least we earn an honest livin' . . . well,' he hesitated, 'some of the time. But them lot'll have picked a good few pockets before the day's out . . . Right, Dolly,' he said, taking the bag of oats off the mare's head, 'that's enough for you, my lovely.' And pushing the bag well under the driver's seat where thieving hands couldn't reach it he picked up the reins and cried, 'Gerrup!'

Dolly was much refreshed after her snack and she set off at a smart trot and would have broken into a canter if Pete hadn't restrained her. 'Whoa!' he laughed. 'Once she's got a bit of grub in her belly she goes along like one o'clock.'

As Dolly drew level with the swells their mood abruptly changed from jocular to truculent and they began to push and shove each other.

'Watch out!' said Clem. But her warning came too late. One of them lost his balance and fell headlong under the back wheels of the cart.

Pete pulled up sharply and Clem screamed.

'You've killed him, you little bwat!' cried a man,

bending over the prostrate body of his friend. 'The poor fellow's dead as a doorknocker.'

'We're in for it now,' muttered Pete through clenched teeth.

'Will they . . . Will they put us in clink?' stammered Clem. 'Will they top us?'

'Nah. After all we didn't rub him out . . . *We didn't*, Clem,' he insisted as she started to shake her head. 'It was his fault, he was larkin' about. The crushers won't do nothin' to us, but them . . .' he shuddered as the swells gathered round the cart ominously, glaring at him and Clem, for he knew their revenge would be swift and brutal.

'I don't think he's pegged out,' said one, staring at the body under the cart. 'I just seen him bweathe . . . Yeh, yeh, he's alive. But only just.'

'I weckon his legs bwoken,' said another. 'It looks kind of bwoken to me.'

'You're wight,' agreed the first. 'You'd best get him to a hospital,' he said to Pete.

'A hospital?' exclaimed Pete in horror. 'But that's where people go to die.'

'And that's what'll happen to our poor fwiend if you don't get a move on,' snapped the man. 'Careful with him,' he admonished the others as they lifted the injured man into the back of the cart.

'And huwwy up,' he said to Pete, 'or it'll be too late.'

'I will, guv, I will,' said Pete, bringing his whip down hard on Dolly's rump. The mare whinnied in distress, for she was not used to harsh treatment from Pete, and took off at a canter.

'Not so fast, Pete, you'll hurt him,' said Clem, looking anxiously at the man lying white-faced and silent among the dirty sacks.

'I got to go fast or he'll croak before we get there.'

'Nah, he's comin' round. He's openin' his eyes. Stop a kick, Pete, and I'll get in the back with him.'

Pete pulled Dolly to a halt and Clem stumbled out of the front seat, hobbled round to the back and hauled herself aboard.

'You all right, mister?' she asked, peering into the man's face.

'Where . . . where am I?' he asked in a faint voice.

'In a cart.'

'Why?'

'We ran over . . . I mean, you *fell* under the wheels. You hurt your leg real bad, so we're takin' you to hospital.'

'Don't do that.' The man reached out to her with a trembling hand. 'Take me home.'

'But your friends said we got to take you to . . .'

'Let me die at home.' The man plucked at Clem's sleeve. 'Please!'

Clem sighed and shook her head. 'He says he wants to go home, Pete.'

'But we were told to . . .'

'I know, I know, but we'd best do as he wants, Pete. Where d'you live, mister?'

The man murmured something, but his voice was so weak Clem could barely hear him.

'Where?' She bent down, her ear close to his mouth.

'What did he say?' asked Pete.

'He said he lives in Walworth.'

'Walworth?' Pete was aghast. 'That's the other side of the river. It'll take ages'n ages to get there.'

'Then let's get goin',' said Clem. 'The sooner we get there the sooner we get back.' And cradling the man's head on her lap to protect him from the jolts as the cart lurched and swayed over the cobblestones she whispered, 'You'll be all right, mister. Pete'll get you home all right.'

Dolly's pace had slowed to a plod by the time they reached Walworth, and Pete was slumped over the reins, struggling to stay awake.

'He still alive?' he asked Clem, nodding at the man.

'Yeh, but I reckon he's fadin' fast.'

'Ask him where he lives.'

'Where's your home, mister?' The man's eyelids flickered. 'I said where's your home?' Clem repeated in a louder voice.

'The Georg'n . . .' The man was clearly too weak to speak and his voice faded away.

'The George'n what, mister?'

'Dwagon.'

'Know where the George'n Dwagon is, Pete?' she said.

'Clem, I never been to Walworth in my whole life. How the devil would I know . . .?'

'Go to the end of this woad, past the bwewewy, down 'Angman's Lane, take a third wight and it's stwaight ahead,' said the man.

'Got that, Pete?' said Clem.

'Nah, I couldn't hear nothin'. What did he say?'

'Go to the end of this woad, past the bwewewy, down—'

'What's the matter with you?' Pete frowned. 'Why you talkin' sappy?'

'I'm just repeatin' what the bloke said,' Clem snapped. 'Down 'Angman's Lane, take a third wight and it's stwaight ahead.'

All was quiet at the George and Dragon when the cart drew up.

'Hold on to me, guv,' Pete said to the man, helping him out of the cart. 'Nah, not her,' he shook his head as the man put his arm around Clem's shoulder. 'She can't . . .'

'Course I can. You lean on me, mister,' said the girl stoutly.

'Oh my leg, my leg,' he groaned as Pete and Clem half carried, half dragged him across the pavement and banged on the side door.

'Louder,' urged the man. 'My . . . er . . . my sister's a heavy sleeper.'

Pete banged on the door again and someone shouted, 'Who is it?'

'It's me – Tom,' said the man in an amazingly strong voice for someone who only minutes before had been close to death.

'Tom!' The bolts were drawn back and a woman threw open the door, her face split in a huge grin. 'Tom, where you been, you old . . . Oh!' Her face fell when she saw Pete and Clem. 'The Terror won't be pleased with them two. The boy's too big to get up chimneys and she's a cripple.'

Pete and Clem were so shocked they stared at the woman, open-mouthed.

'Best I could do, Nell. But I got their horse and cart as well – though it's made a fwightful mess of my twucks,' fretted Tom, rubbing at the soot on his check trousers.

'All right,' said Nell. And grabbing Clem by the hair she yanked her in. Pete lunged at the man, but his broken leg seemed to have miraculously mended itself and after the briefest of scuffles Pete too was hurled into the passageway.

'I'll go'n look for somethin' better, Nell,' said Tom. And he strode away, whistling a merry tune.

'You two follow me,' snapped Nell, locking and bolting the door.

'We're not goin' nowhere,' retorted Pete.

'Oh, you are, young sir,' she cackled, pinching Pete's cheek so hard he yelped. 'You're goin' straight to the bottom of the river, you are. *And* your little friend,' she added, leering at Clem. 'Food for fishes, the pair of you!'

32

Billy was utterly lost. He had spent most of that miserable night wandering up and down streets, stumbling into darkened courtyards, tripping over the bodies of sleeping tramps, running away from thieves and drunkards, leaping aside as buckets of rubbish or chamber-pot slops streamed in a filthy shower from upper windows, and getting colder and wearier and hungrier with every passing hour.

At last, exhausted, he had stumbled into the gutter, curled into a tight ball, fallen asleep and dreamed he was standing in front of a pork pie as big as a house. It had a front door and windows and a golden, glazed roof that was crimped round the edges. His mouth watering, he opened the door in the crust and was just about to sink his teeth into the pink gristle inside when a hand grabbed his shoulder and pulled him back, shaking him hard.

'Nah!' he cried. 'Get off! It's mine, I found it first!'

'Did you, indeed?' drawled a strangely familiar

voice. 'And there I was thinkin' the gutter belonged to evewybody.'

Billy sat up and peered sleepily at the man leaning over him, a very handsome, elegant young man in his cutaway jacket and richly brocaded waistcoat.

'Here, I know you,' he cried. 'You're old Ramsbum.'

'It's Wams*bottom*,' Tom retorted. 'And who the devil are you? Oh . . . Oh yeh, I wemember now,' he drawled, putting a monocle to his eye. 'You're one of the little varmints I met in that slum, Devil's Acre.'

'You tried to grab me. You . . .'

'Course I didn't,' Tom shrugged. 'I was just larkin' about. Is it my fault if you don't have a sense of humour, Mr . . . Bless me if I can wemember your name. Perks, Perky . . .?'

'Perkinski.'

'Perkin*ski*! Of course. How could I forget anythin' so widiculous,' Tom sneered. 'And how is *Madam Natasha*?'

'Who?'

'Your gwanmother. Still tellin' a pack of lies, is she? Still puttin' a load of muck in bottles and sellin' it as magic potions?'

'Yeh.' Billy nodded.

'And what bwings you to this part of the met-wopolis then?'

'Eh?'

'What you doin' here?'

Billy was so pleased to find someone he knew he had quite forgotten about the horrors of the night. But suddenly they all came tumbling back into his mind, the sight of Mr Bullock and the Mateys running away from the policemen, the headlong flight through the dark, stinking alleyways, the fear, the loneliness . . .

He burst into tears.

'What's wong, young'un?' Tom put a hand on his shoulder.

'I'm lost.'

'Where are your thievin' bwothers?'

'Don't know.' Billy's sobs grew louder.

'What about your ma and pa?'

'I lost them too.'

Tom's eyes lit up and he stared at Billy like a cat eyeing a particularly juicy little bird. 'You mean nobody knows where you are?'

The little boy shook his head.

'Well, you'd better come along with me then. I know a place where they got a nice warm fire and plenty to eat. Like that, would you?'

Billy stopped crying for a moment and stared at the man intently. He hadn't eaten for such a long time his stomach hurt.

'They got pork pies, mister?' he asked.

'They certainly have. Biggest, tastiest pies this side of the Thames.'

'And tripe and onions?'

'Softest, whitest twipe you ever sunk your teeth into.'

'And gingerbread nuts?'

'Many as you can eat.'

'And will you take me home afterwards?'

'Course I will.'

'Promise?'

'Slit my thwoat, hope to cwoak if I don't.'

'Righto.' Billy reached up and took the man's outstretched hand.

33

'If I don't get somethin' in my belly soon, Jem, I'm goin' to peg out,' complained Ned.

'Yeh, we got to get out of here.'

'Oh, don't start that again.'

'I thought of a way.'

'What?'

'Climb up them sacks and break the glass in that.' Jem pointed to the small window close to the ceiling.

'Don't be a stupe. That window's got more bars on it than Newgate prison. How you goin' to get through them?'

'I'm not. You are.'

'Don't be daft. Who d'you think I am, Jack Sheppard? Anyway, why me?'

'Cos you're skinnier than me.'

'I'm not.'

'You are. You're so thin you could slip through the holes of a sieve.'

'Why don't you send Alfie up? He's half my size.'

'Cos he isn't here, is he? He's upstairs workin'. Look, it's dead easy, Ned. All you got to do is hunch your shoulders and wriggle your . . .'

'Nah, I'm not goin' up them sacks. I'll fall and break my neck.'

'Course you won't. Come on,' said Jem, pulling him to his feet.

'Nah!' Ned fought to free himself. 'Nah, I won't. I can't.'

'Well, as I see it you got three choices – you can stay here and starve to death or get chucked in the river or you can try and get out that window.'

'Er . . .' Ned looked at it doubtfully.

'Righto, stay here,' said Jem, crossing his arms.

'Nah, I'll . . . I'll try. But what do I do when . . . *if* I get out the window?'

'Go round to the front door, sneak in when nobody's lookin' and come down here and let me out.'

'Just like that?' said Ned, shaking his head in disbelief.

'What d'you mean?'

'That window's up in the roof. How'm I goin' to get down the other side?'

'Jump.'

'And break my neck?'

'Ned, you got . . .'

'I know, I know. I got three choices. I can starve, drown or break my neck. Oh well,' he shrugged, 'since I'm goin' to die anyway I might as well do it the quickest.'

'Jammy!' exclaimed Jem, well pleased with his brother's decision. 'Now grab hold of the sacks and stick your toes in like you were climbin' up a wall with cracks in it.'

Gingerly Ned began to climb while Jem watched from below.

'You're doin' all right,' Jem said encouragingly.

'Nah, I'm not.'

'You are. You're almost there.'

'I only just started.'

'You're gettin' the hang of it now.'

'I keep slippin'.'

'You're nearly at the top.'

'I can't hold on.'

'Just a bit more.'

'I . . . I . . . Blimey, I done it! I done it!' cried Ned, heaving himself on to the top of the pile.

'Told you you could,' cried Jem, punching the air. 'Told you . . .! Hey up, there's someone comin'. Keep your head down, Ned, and don't say nothin'.'

The next moment the bolts on the door were drawn back and Nell came in pushing a boy and girl ahead of her.

'Got a little present for you two . . .' She stopped, frowning. 'Where's the other one, your pesky brother?' she snapped at Jem.

Jem stared at the floor.

'Where is that brat?' Nell demanded, walking round the cellar and kicking the sacks as hard as she could. 'I said, *Where is he?*'

'I don't know,' muttered Jem. 'I think he must've gone.'

'Gone? Don't be a fool, nobody can get out of here. Not alive, anyway. If you don't tell me where he is, I'll . . .' Before Jem could duck she grabbed his ear and twisted it so hard that for one moment he thought she'd wrenched it clean off his head.

'Tell me! Tell me!' she screeched, as the boy grimaced in pain.

'I'm up here,' shouted Ned, peering over the top of the sacks.

'Oh, right. Went for a little climb, did we? Wanted to see the view from the ceilin'?' said Nell. 'Well, I want you down here. Now!' And she launched herself at the pile of sacks and began to jerk them back and forth.

Jem watched in horror as the pile swayed slowly, slowly, like a tree in the wind, then faster, faster . . .

'Don't!' shouted Ned. 'Nell, don't. Please!'

'Come on down, darlin',' she laughed, pushing the sacks harder until the boy lost his balance and toppled to the floor with a bone-crunching thwack!

'Aargh!' he groaned. 'I think I broke somethin'.'

'Good,' smiled Nell. 'Pity you didn't break everythin'.'

'You all right, Ned?' said Jem, helping him to his feet when the woman had gone.

'My arm feels a bit funny, my elbow looks as if it's on back to front . . . Jem, who're they?' he whispered, nodding at the boy and girl who were staring at them intently.

'Probably a couple of kids workin' for the Terror,' he whispered back.

'Nah, we're not,' said the boy.

'Who are you then?'

'Who are you?'

'I asked first.'

'I'm Pete. And she's Clem.'

'Well, I'm Jem. And he's my brother Ned.'

'What're you doin' here?'

'What're *you* doin' here?'

'I asked first.'

'We're lookin' for my brother.'

'Well, we're looking for a kid that works with us, only he ran away.'

'So why'd you come here?'

'Cos a bloke tricked us.'

'Tricked you?' Jem scoffed. 'Lor, nobody's never taken me for a mug. I'm too fly for that.'

'So why did you come here?' said Pete, bridling.

'Cos our gran talks to spirits,' Ned blurted out before Jem could stop him. 'And they told her that Bil . . .'

'Spirits? Your gran talks to *spirits*? Crikey,' Pete nearly choked himself laughing, 'you must be a couple of stupes to believe that.'

'Who you callin' a stupe, crumpet-face?' snarled Jem.

Now Pete was not a vain boy, although if anyone had asked him he would have described himself as 'uncommon handsome', but he was very sensitive about his pitted and pock-marked skin.

'None of your lip, shrimp!' he retorted.

Jem flushed. It was a source of great distress to him that, try as he might, he didn't seem to grow — not upwards, anyway. To add insult to injury his brother was a year younger and more than an inch taller. And the sight of Ned sniggering at Pete's insult heated Jem's anger to boiling point.

He paused for a moment, deliberating which of the two to flatten first. Then with a muttered, 'I'll get you later!' to Ned, he set about Pete with fists and feet.

34

'We there yet, mister?' demanded Billy. 'I'm near starvin'.'

'Not far now,' said Tom.

'Is it your home?'

'In a manner of speakin'.'

'Eh?'

'I live there with my uncle. Nice bloke,' Tom sniggered. 'He loves little kids like you.'

'Will he give me eggs and bacon?'

'Eggs, bacon, kippers, kidneys, anythin' you want – a feast fit for a king. There we are.' Tom stopped and pointed at the George and Dragon.

'Cor!' Billy was impressed. 'Your uncle must be uncommon rich to live in a place like that, mister. Are all them people goin' in his friends?'

'They are,' Tom grinned. 'And so are all the ones comin' out. He's got lots of fwiends.'

'Could I be his friend, mister?'

'Course you could. I weckon you and my uncle'll be fwiends till the day you die . . . Which pwobably won't be long,' Tom added under his breath.

35

The two boys were evenly matched and the fight raged on to cries of, 'Stop it, Pete. Don't be so daft,' from Clem and, 'Go on, Jem. Give him one in the eye,' from Ned.

At the height of the battle, when Jem was re-arranging Pete's teeth and Pete was remodelling Jem's nose, the door opened and Nell came in, pushing a small boy ahead of her, his bright-blue eyes staring out of a soot-covered face.

Immediately Jem and Pete sprang apart, wiping their bloodied faces on dirty sleeves.

'Here's another brat to keep you company. Go on!' said Nell, jabbing the boy in the back.

'But I haven't had my eggs'n bacon yet,' he whined, hugging her knees and looking up at her beseechingly. 'And what about my pork pie? Tom said I'd get a feast.'

'And so you will, my ducky. See them?' She pointed at the hordes of cockroaches that were scuttling across the floor and up the walls. 'You can eat as many of them as you like.'

'Don't want them,' sobbed the little boy. 'Want eggs'n bacon. Want a pork pie. Want . . .'

'Blimey, it's Billy,' said Jem.

'Billy!' cried the others.

The little boy turned round and looked at them in amazement – and then his grimy face split into a huge smile. 'Jem!' he cried, hurling himself at his brother. 'And Ned and . . . Cor, it's Pete and Clem too. What're you all doin' here?'

'Never mind what we're doin' here, where've you been?' said Jem. 'Pa's been lookin' for you all over London.'

'I been with them.' Billy pointed at Pete and Clem. 'Least I was.'

Jem's mouth dropped open. '*Them?*'

'Yeh, I was livin' with—'

'Hold your jaw, you clack box!' said Nell, raising her hand to hit him.

'Leave him alone,' cried Ned, pulling Billy away. 'Don't you touch my brother.'

'Your brother? Oh, so this is the famous Billy, is it? Well, well, so now we got all three of you. Aren't we the lucky ones?' chuckled Nell. 'Right, upstairs you two,' she snapped at Jem and Ned. 'And quick

about it. The dog'n rat match is startin' any time now.'

'Nah, don't leave me,' cried Billy, clinging to them. 'Don't leave me.'

'Stop that,' scolded Nell, 'or I'll give you a good jacketin'.'

'Come here, nipper,' said Clem, putting an arm around Billy and drawing him close to her. 'You stay with Pete'n me. You'll be all right.'

'Ah, ain't she a sweet little mum,' sneered Nell.

'We'll be back in a kick, Billy,' said Jem. 'And we'll bring you some grub.'

'Promise?'

'Honour bright,' said Jem, crossing his fingers behind his back.

36

The two boys followed Nell up the stairs and through the swing doors into the main saloon. The long bar was crowded with men and women from almost every walk of life: costermongers with brightly coloured scarves knotted around their necks, their greasy ringlets twisted back over their ears; shopkeepers, some of them still wearing aprons; coach drivers in livery; soldiers in uniforms; even some wealthy people and aristocrats in fashionable clothes. Most were smoking pipes or cigars, and under their arms or tied to the legs of their chairs were their dogs, many with vicious gashes on their faces and bodies, where they had come off worse in a fight.

'I reckon Beauty here's goin' to wipe the floor with your lot,' boasted one man, stroking the enormous head of a slobbering bulldog. 'Only last week he killed more than fifty rats in half an hour.' And he looked around with a 'Beat that!' expression.

'Fifty? Is that all?' drawled Tom Ramsbottom, who was leaning nonchalantly against the bar. 'I weckon the poor cweature must be half dead himself if he's that slow . . .' And he paused for the inevitable shouts of laughter that rang round the room. 'Now my dog,' he picked up an ugly little terrier with a mouth that stretched from ear to ear, 'this clever little fellow's killed a *hundwed* in half and hour.'

There were murmurs of astonishment and admiration. But the owner of the bulldog turned red with indignation. 'I'll wager you Beauty can kill more rats in half an hour than your puny little runt,' he growled.

'And what will you wager . . .? Not that neckerchief, thank you.' Tom flicked it disdainfully. 'It's a cheap thing and it ain't fashionable. I wouldn't be seen dead in it, fwankly.'

The bulldog owner leaped off his stool, incensed.

'I'll wager you this,' he cried, pulling a handsome ring off his finger. 'Twenty-four carat Welsh gold this is,' he said, holding it up for everyone to see. 'It belonged to my father.'

'Oh, all wight,' said Tom. 'And I'll bet you . . .'

'My gran's pearl brooch,' Jem shouted.

'What . . .?' Tom spun round.

'The one you nicked from her.'

'Lor', bless us!' Tom drawled. 'Gen'lemen, I'd like you all to meet Mr Perkin*ski*.'

'Mr What*ski*?' shouted someone at the back.

This was greeted with howls of laughter.

'Mr Perkin*ski*'s a genuine gypsy – or so he says,' Tom added with a sneer.

'And I'd like you all to meet The Hon Ramsbottom, the son of a duke . . . *or so he says*,' Jem scoffed. 'And don't take nothin' from him for a bet neither,' he turned to the owner of the bulldog, 'cos if it's anythin' like the *gold* watch and the *diamond* pin I nicked from him it's a load of old rubbish.'

Tom turned all shades of red from deep pink to crimson and lunged at Jem with flying fists. But Jem ducked and butted him in the stomach and the two of them fell to the floor, pounding each other, while hands reached out to dissuade Ned from joining in.

'What's this shindy? What's goin' on?' came a sinister voice from the door.

Immediately the room fell deathly quiet.

'It's nothin', guv'nor,' said Tom, scrambling to his feet and adjusting his jacket and cravat.

'Nothin'?' The Terror squinted at him. 'Sounded more than nothin' to me. Know these two, do you?' He nodded at Jem and Ned.

'Er . . . Nah, never seen them in my life, guv'nor.'

'That's a whopper!' shouted Jem, struggling to free himself from a burly man who had pinned his arms behind his back. 'He stole my gran's pearl brooch. And it was a real pearl too, not like the bit of tin and glass I nicked from him.'

'*What* did you say?' The Terror bent down, putting his face so close to Jem's the boy could almost see his brains through his open nostrils.

'I said it was a b . . . bit of tin and . . .'

'*You* nicked somethin' from *Tom*?'

Jem nodded.

'That true, Tom.' The Terror turned to him.

'Well . . . In a manner of speakin', guv'nor . . . I mean . . .'

'DID HE?'

'Yeh.' Tom squirmed under the man's piercing gaze. 'Yeh, as a matter of fact, he did. But I was a bit peaky at the time and there were ten of them and . . .'

'Whoa, that's another whacker,' protested Jem. 'There was just Ned and me and my little brother.'

'Well, well.' The Terror turned his gaze on the boy. 'I got to congratulate you, I have. I didn't think nobody could get the better of my nephew. I brought him up to be the best pickpocket in London. At least he *was*,' he added with a wicked smile.

The young man flinched.

'You're a clever lad,' the Terror said to Jem. 'You got a bright future in front of you. Tell you what, I'm goin' to let you work for me alongside Tom.'

'I'd . . . I'd rather go home, Your Honour.'

'Rather go home?' said the Terror with a pained expression. 'Why? Is there somethin' wrong with the accommodation here?' A nervous titter went round the room as if people weren't sure whether to laugh or not. 'Well, if you don't like it where you are, son, then I'll put you in with the rats. I reckon you'll be nice and comfortable with them.'

He turned to Nell, who put her hands on her hips and rocked back and forth with laughter as if it were the funniest joke she'd ever heard. The men and women around the bar obligingly followed suit.

'And what about you?' The Terror turned his piercing gaze on Ned. 'You want to go home too, do you?'

'Nah, I mean yeh, I mean I'm n . . . no use to you, guv,' stammered Ned. 'I'm no good at nickin' things like Jem.'

'Pity.' The Terror stroked his chin thoughtfully. 'Then I'll just have to dump you in the river, I'm afraid, cos I got no use for kids that can't nick stuff.'

37

'I been lookin' in my crystal ball, Bert,' said Gran.

'Oh yeh? And what did you see this time, Billy flyin' through the air on a chimney brush?' said Pa caustically.

'I saw him with Jem and Ned,' snapped the old woman. 'They were runnin' up some stairs like mad and screamin'.'

'Well, they'll scream all the louder when I get hold of them,' Pa growled. 'I'm not blamin' Billy, cos he's so daft he couldn't find his way out of a chamber pot, but the other two . . .' he shook his head. 'They shouldn't have gone off like that without tellin' me.'

'Where were they, Gran?' asked Ma Perkinski.

'I told you, runnin' up some stairs . . .'

'Yeh, but what stairs in what house in what street?'

'It wasn't a house. It was a pub.'

'A pub?' Ma said eagerly. 'What was its name?'

'Don't know, I couldn't see it.'

'Oh well, that makes it dead easy,' sneered Pa. 'All I got to do is go in every pub in London and ask them if they've seen my boys.'

'I told you it's in Walworth,' said Gran, sounding exasperated. 'I told you a dozen times that the Walworth Ter—'

'Oh, don't start all that hornswoggle about the Walworth Terror again,' said Pa.

38

The Terror sat hunched over a table by the entrance to the George and Dragon with Old Jack at his side and Delilah at his feet. The ugly brute watched the customers as venomously as its master and snarled, baring its fangs in greeting whenever the door opened and more people piled into the hot, smoky room.

With a nod to Old Jack and a sideways glance at the Terror, the customers put their entrance money on the table. In no time at all the pile of gold and silver coins had risen to an impressive height.

The clock over the bar chimed out the hour and the Terror signalled to Nell who, grabbing Jem and Ned by the scruff of their necks, dragged them across the room.

'You ready to start work, gen'lemen?' he enquired. 'Now, I just want to remind you, if you ever tell anyone what you seen here today, I'll . . .'

'Nah, we won't. We won't tell nobody, Your

Lordship. We can keep a secret,' said Jem, because he knew the dog-and-rat sport was illegal.

'And you think I'm balmy enough to believe you, do you?' jeered the Terror.

'Ain't this wet? Ain't this dry? Cut my throat if I tell a lie,' chanted Jem.

'Oh, don't worry, lad, I will. I'll slit it from one ear to the other. And you'd better not try to make a run for it, neither.'

'Nah, we wouldn't, guv,' said Ned.

'*Nah, we wouldn't, guv.*' The Terror opened his eyes wide and shook his head furiously, aping the frightened boy. 'Course you wouldn't. But just to make doubly sure I'm goin' to tell my dogs to keep an eye on you . . . Where's the other kid, Nell, the boy?'

'Alfie? He's in the kitchen, scrubbin' the floor, Terror. But it's all right, Samson's watchin' him,' she added quickly, as his face clouded over. 'He won't let the scamp get away. You know what happened last time he tried. He . . .'

'Stop clackin', woman, and throw the brat back in the cellar. I want Samson here to watch these two. Him and Delilah'll make sure they don't do nothin' foolish, won't you, my sweet?'

The dog looked up at him with adoring eyes.

'Are all bets placed then, gen'lemen?' cried the

landlord. 'This is your last chance. Place your bets now, please.'

'Right, Jack, go and get the rats.' The Terror turned to the old man. 'We'll be startin' in a few minutes.'

'Come with me, lads,' said Old Jack, leading Jem and Ned back down the stairs to the far end of the dark passageway, where he drew a key from his waist-coat pocket and opened the door to the rat cellar.

The boys fell back against the wall, aghast. Though they were used to the foul smells of London, the stench that came from the long, narrow cellar was like every disgusting smell in the world rolled into one.

Ned clamped a hand over his mouth but Jem was made of sterner stuff and he followed the old man into the cellar, which was full of rusty iron cages, stacked right up to the ceiling, every one filled to the brim with a seething, squirming mass of small animals.

'They know what's goin' to happen to them', said Old Jack, as the squealing increased to a deafen-ing din. 'They're very intelligent creatures, rats . . . more's the pity. They got as good a brain as any dog. Better, I'd say. And they got feelin's too. I reckon they feel pain as much as we do.'

Jem frowned. 'Well, if you think that why d'you let the dogs kill them?'

The old man's shoulders slumped. 'Don't have much choice, do I? I'm old, I can't work – not proper work any more; I got no home, no place to go – unless I go in the workhouse.' He shuddered. 'At least I got a roof over my head and grub in my belly as long as I look after these rats for the Terror . . . Come on, lad,' he beckoned to Ned who was hanging behind.

'D'you have a match every week?' said Jem, following the old man as he edged past the cages.

'Every Sunday, come rain or shine – but we keep quiet about it,' he said, putting a finger to his lips. 'If a crusher happens along we tell him it's just a meetin' of dog fanciers and––'

'Jack!' Nell shouted from the top of the stairs. 'Hurry up! The Terror's waitin' and he's in no mood for nonsense, I can tell you.'

'Go on then, lads, carry them cages up to the pit room, sharp like,' said the old man.

'Where's the pit room, guv?'

'Right above the bar. There's a secret staircase behind a panel in the wall. All you got to do is press the––'

'Jack! For pity's sake!' Nell sounded beside herself with anxiety.

'Comin', comin', my lovely,' he called. 'Don't you fret yourself.'

'Ned,' Jem whispered in his brother's ear. 'This is our chance.'

'Chance?' Ned frowned.

'To escape.'

'You off your chump? What with Nell and the Terror upstairs and this old codger down here, not to mention them varminty dogs,' Ned looked fearfully at Samson and Delilah, who sat in the doorway watching their every move, 'we're never goin' to get out of here – leastways, not alive.'

'Just listen, will you? I'll keep Old Jack talkin' and when he's not lookin' you open all the cages quick as you can and let the rats out.'

'What?' Ned felt every hair on the back of his neck stand up.

'It's our only hope.'

'But . . .'

'D'you want to get out or not?'

'But them rats . . .'

'It's them rats or the bottom of the river with your throat cut.'

'What're you two clackin' about?' frowned Old Jack, cupping his hand to his ear. 'Speak up, will you, I can't hear so well no more.'

 243

'I was just sayin' to Ned as how I wish we had some real big rats to take up to the pit,' said Jem. 'These are all littl'uns,' he added contemptuously, peering into the cages where the small creatures huddled together. 'Haven't you got nothin' better?'

The old man frowned. 'You watch your tongue,' he grunted. 'They're good rats, they are.'

'But you must have some with a bit more fight in them, guv,' insisted Jem. 'What about them in the corner?' he pointed.

'Ah, I see you got a good eye for this kind of job, youngster. I picked them up last night. Real plummy, aren't they?'

'Blow me tight, look at the teeth on them,' said Jem, working his way towards the cages with Old Jack in tow. 'Ned! Ned!' Jem hissed over his shoulder, nodding at the cages. 'Go on!'

'What?' Old Jack cupped his hand to his ear again.

'I was just tellin' my brother not to get so close',' shouted Jem, 'He keeps steppin' on my heels.'

Ned wavered for a moment – but only a moment. Much as he feared the rats, he feared a wet grave even more. While the old man chattered away the boy set to work behind his back, darting from cage to cage, opening the catches and throwing back the lids while the Terror's two dogs sat in the doorway watching with interest.

Within minutes Ned had opened dozens of cages and the little creatures, seizing their chance to escape, swarmed down the sides, dropped to the floor and scuttled out into the passageway and up the stairs.

Samson and Delilah snapped at them, killing a dozen or so, but others ran up their legs and sank their teeth into the dogs' noses and ears. Enraged, the dogs shook their heads furiously, but the rats hung on, biting all the harder. In no time at all the beleaguered animals realized the odds were heavily against them and, throwing loyalty to the wind, they tucked their tails between their legs and fled.

Meanwhile Old Jack, unaware of the chaos behind his back, was telling Jem about the time he had chased a rat as big as a cat through the sewers.

'Led me a merry dance, it did. But I got the little varmint in the end,' he laughed, as Ned frantically tore open cage after cage, tipping the rats to the floor.

Hundreds of them were now free and they began swarming up the stairs and into the bar. People screamed and ran, colliding with each other and tripping over dogs that had broken free and were racing around like demons, barking and snapping at everything in sight.

The Terror leaped to his feet with a bellow of rage and overturned the table on which the entrance money was stacked in large piles.

'Come on, Ned, you've done enough!' shouted Jem, running out of the rat cellar.

'Here, where'd you think you're goin'?' cried Old Jack. He turned round then and seeing nearly all the cages empty let out a great cry of anguish.

'My babies! Where are my babies?'

Jem and Ned raced through the dimly lit passage-ways beneath the pub and when they came to the cellar where Billy, Pete and Clem were imprisoned they drew back the bolts and threw open the door.

'Run! Run!' they yelled. 'Plaguy quick!'

Pete shot up. 'What's happenin'?' he said.

'You're free!'

'But . . .'

'Come on!' And grabbing Billy's arm Jem yanked him up the stairs.

'You all right, Clem?' said Pete, picking up Alfie.

'Course I am,' she grinned. 'Never better.'

'Cor!' exclaimed the boys as they all emerged from the stairwell into the saloon. 'What a sight for sore eyes.'

And indeed it was. The Terror was on his hands and knees, scrabbling for the coins that had spilt all over the floor, Nell was on a chair screaming blue murder, her skirt and petticoat hoisted around her waist as rats ran up and down her legs, and Tom was trying to brush off a particularly determined couple, which had taken a fancy to his cravat and were chewing it vigorously. Above it all Old Jack could be heard crying piteously, 'My babies! My babies!'

Somebody finally wrenched open the street door and a swarm of people, dogs and rats burst out – to be greeted by the horrified shrieks of passers-by.

There was the deafening sound of rattles being furiously spun and five or six burly policemen came charging down the street at full gallop.

'What on earth's happening?' cried an old lady cringing in a doorway.

'Reckon we've happened on a dog and rat match, missus,' replied one of the men as he ran past. 'And from the look of it the rats have come off best for once.'

39

Uncle Arthur came running into Devil's Acre looking excited. 'I got some news,' he cried.

'Yeh, so have we,' said Pa dolefully.

'We've lost Jem and Ned now,' said Ma, her face the picture of misery.

'What?' Uncle Arthur stopped dead. 'Don't tell me they been snatched too?'

'Nah,' said Pa, 'I doubt it. Jem's too fly for that. They left early in the mornin' before we were up and we didn't think nothin' of it cos sometimes they get workin' real early, but when they didn't come back at night we twigged they'd gone lookin' for Billy.'

'That's what I come to tell you about,' said Uncle Arthur. 'That's my good news. Your Billy's been seen in Walworth. He was seen walkin' with one of the swell mob, hand in hand, very friendly like . . . What's wrong? I thought you'd be pleased.'

'Walworth,' said Pa, aghast.

'Yeh, Walworth.'

'That's where the . . . the Terror hangs out,' whispered Ma, her face ashen.

'Yeh, he does . . . Oh.' It was Uncle Arthur's turn to look aghast. 'I just remembered somethin' . . . Oh, Lor'! Jem and Ned were askin' me about the Walworth Terror. You don't think they've . . .?'

Pa sank his head in his hands. 'It's all my fault,' he groaned. 'Gran kept tellin' me the Terror'd got Billy, but I didn't believe her. I just laughed at her. I said it was a load of hornwoggle . . .'

'Don't blame yourself, love,' said Ma, putting a hand on his shoulder. 'Nobody never believes nothin' Gran says. She's always makin' things up.'

'But this time, just this once, she was right,' sighed Uncle Arthur, sitting down next to his brother and sinking his head in his hands too. 'The Terror *has* got Billy – and he'll have Jem and Ned too. I'm sorry,' he said, as Ma wrung her hands in agony, 'I told them not to go nowhere near him.'

'Yeh, but you know what Jem's like,' said Pa gruffly. 'You tell him to do one thing and sure as life he'll do another.'

'So, what're you goin' to do now, Bert?'

'I'm goin' to Walworth, of course.'

'*What?*' Uncle Arthur could hardly believe his ears. 'They're my kids, my flesh and blood,' said Pa stoutly. 'And if the Terror's got them I'm goin' to get them back.'

'You'll be careful, won't you, Bert,' said Ma anxiously as her husband pulled on his jacket and rammed a hat firmly on his bald head. 'I don't want you endin' up in the river too.'

'Don't you worry, my precious,' he said. 'It'd take more than the Terror to get the better of me.'

'How you goin' to get there, Bert?' asked Uncle Arthur.

'Walk, of course.'

'Don't be daft, Walworth's the other side of the world.'

'You been there, have you?'

'Yeh, I went there once years ago to look at a donkey, took me hours'n hours, I thought my trotters'd drop off.'

'I'd best take one of them omnibuses then.'

'An omnibus?' Uncle Arthur's eyebrows shot up. 'That don't come cheap, Bert.'

'I know, but I got to get there plaguy quick.'

'Here,' Uncle Arthur reached into his pocket and drew out some coins. 'Take this . . .'

'Nah, it's all right, Arthur,' said Pa, waving his hand away. 'I'll take somethin' from the money the family gave me for Billy's ransom.'

40

'Not so fast,' cried Pete as he and Jem and Ned hurried away from the George and Dragon, looking fearfully over their shoulders in case they were being followed. 'Clem can't keep up.' He lowered his voice so the girl wouldn't hear, 'She's got a game leg.'

'Ned,' said Jem as they stopped running, 'where's Billy?'

'I thought he was with you.'

'Nah, he let go of my hand. I thought he was with you . . . Oh, blimey!' Jem cried in dismay. 'Don't tell me we lost him again, just when we found him.'

'He must still be in the George'n Dragon.'

'I'll have to go back and get him then,' said Jem with a sinking heart.

'I'll go with you.'

'Nah, you stay here. If them crushers catch us they'll put the bracelets on us and cart us off to prison. No point in us both doin' time.'

'But why should we do time?' protested Ned. 'We didn't do nothin' wrong.'

'Don't make no difference,' said Pete. 'Jem's right, they'll collar you anyway just cos you worked for the Terror.'

'You lot wait for me here,' said Jem, turning to go. 'And if I'm not back with Billy in half an hour, scarper.'

In his haste to get back to the George and Dragon Jem almost blundered into a man standing on a ladder painting Harris & Sons in bright red letters above his shop window.

'Lucky I saw you in time, my lad, or you'd have had this lot all over you,' he said, pointing to his paint pot.

'Not my fault,' grumbled Jem. 'You shouldn't leave your pesky ladder on the pavement for people to trip over.' And he walked on.

A big crowd had now gathered outside the pub, and as Jem drew near he saw Nell, Old Jack, Tom Ramsbottom and the landlord, all handcuffed to constables and being hustled into the back of a cart. A loud cheer went up and there were cries of, 'Chuck them in the drink!' and, 'Hang the lot of them!'

Jem stood on tiptoe, hoping for a glimpse of the Terror, but there were too many people around the cart, brandishing their fists and jumping up and down in a frenzy.

When the villains had been carted off with most of the crowd in tow a few people lingered behind, peering through the windows of the pub and hovering around the door.

'Move along now, ladies and gents,' said one of the policemen who had been left to guard the premises. 'Move along or you'll be arrested for loitering.'

'Oh, crimes!' groaned Jem, peering round the corner. 'How am I goin' to get Billy out with them two crushers standin' by the door?'

And then he had an idea.

41

'Why's Jem takin' so long?' Clem asked for the umpteenth time, looking anxiously down the streeet. 'It's nigh on half hour since he went.'

'He probably can't find Billy,' said Pete. 'The kid might be hidin' somewhere.'

'Or he's been collared,' muttered Ned.

'And maybe Jem's been collared too,' said Pete.

'Nah, don't say that,' Clem rebuked him. 'Jem's a fly bloke, he wouldn't let himself get col . . . What's wrong with them?' she frowned as a dozen or so men and women appeared at the far end of the street chattering like a troupe of frightened monkeys.

'What's up?' Pete called out as they got closer.

'It's the Terror . . . got away . . . he's on the loose,' babbled a woman, drawing her shawl more closely around her shoulders as if to protect herself. 'They copped all the others, took them to the lock-up, but *he* scarpered.'

'I hear as how a couple of kids set all them rats

free,' said a man. 'I wouldn't like to be in their shoes, I'm tellin' you,' he shuddered. 'The Terror'll be lookin' for them. And when he finds them . . .' He hurried on, leaving the threat hanging in the air.

Ned turned deathly white. 'Oh, Lor',' he muttered, looking around nervously as if he expected the Terror to pounce on him at any moment. 'Oh, crimes.'

'Jem . . .' whispered Clem. 'Jem's all by himself.'

'I'll go,' said Ned. 'I'll . . .'

'Nah.' Pete pushed him back. 'I'll go. The Terror's not lookin' for me on account of he's never clapped eyes on me. You stay here and look after Clem and Alfie.' And before Ned could protest Pete had gone, running like the wind to warn Jem he was in terrible danger.

42

'Oh, it's you again, is it?' said the man painting the sign above his shop window. 'Well, hook it!'

'All right, don't get snaggy,' said Jem. 'I only came back to help you.'

'I don't want no help, thank you. I can do it well enough on my own.'

'I just wanted to tell you it doesn't look right to me,' said Jem, surveying the sign with a critical eye. 'That word,' he pointed, 'it's slanting-dicular.'

The man leaned back and squinted at it. 'Looks straight enough to me.'

'Nah, it kind of goes up at the end. You'd see it better if you were down here.'

'Oh, all right.' With a sigh the man began to descend the ladder.

'Here, let me give you a hand,' said Jem helpfully. And reaching up he grabbed the pot and tipped it. A torrent of red paint cascaded over his wideawake and dripped on to his jacket and trousers.

'Now look what you've done!' cried the man angrily.

'What I done? What you done, you mean. I was only tryin' to help and you tipped the varminty pot all over me. Look at my togs. They're ruined.'

'Ruined?' scoffed the man. 'How could I ruin a load of dirty old rags held together with bits of string?'

'These are my best togs,' exclaimed Jem indignantly. 'I reckon you should give me a shillin' or two to buy new ones.'

'Get off!' shouted the man, waving the empty pot at him. 'Get off or I'll . . .!'

Jem ran, wiping his hands in the red paint as he went and smearing it over his face and neck. When he drew near the George and Dragon he started to wave his arms and scream at the top of his lungs, 'Help! Help! Murder! Murder!'

'What's happened?' cried the constables.

'My pa, my pa . . . he's gone ravin' mad . . . got a big axe . . . chopped my ma and all my brothers and sisters into little bits. He tried to get me.' Jem spread his arms wide to show them his blood-stained clothes. 'If you don't stop him he'll chop up my poor old gran and grandpa . . . And the neighbours,' he added for good measure.

'Where d'you live?'

'House just past the dairy. You can't miss it. There's blood drippin' down the walls, gallons of it.'

'You stay here, son. You'll be safer.'

And, waving their night sticks and spinning their rattles, the two policemen set off at the double.

43

Pa got off the bus in Walworth and asked a man selling jellied eels from a cart how to get to the George and Dragon.

'Go to the end of this road, past the brewery, down 'Angman's Lane, take a third right and you'll see it straight ahead,' said the man. 'And remember, I said third *right*, not left.'

'I'm not half baked,' said Pa irritably. 'I do know my left from my right.' And down the road he went, past the brewery, down Hangman's Lane and took a third left.

'Oh, drat!' he groaned. 'I'm lost. That pesky man gave me the wrong directions. Oy, missus,' he shouted at a woman down on her hands and knees scrubbing her doorstep, 'd'you know where the George'n Dragon is?'

'Do I look like a signboard?' she shouted back.

'What's that supposed to mean?'

'Everybody seems to think I got nothin' better to

do than tell them how to get to the George'n Dragon,' she snapped, picking up her bucket and sloshing the contents into the gutter, narrowly missing Pa's trousers. 'Go back down here to the main road and it's starin' you in the face.'

'That's where the Terror hangs out, isn't it?'

The woman looked at him askance. 'He did.'

'So where is he now?'

'You'd best ask the devil that,' she said. And picking up her bucket she went into her house and shut the door.

Muttering about how rude the people of Walworth were, Pa was about to walk on when a boy came hurtling round the corner and knocked him flat.

'Sorry, guv'!' he cried as Pa landed with a resounding thud on his backside.

'Here, you!' Pa bellowed, scrambling to his feet. 'Come back here, you varmint. I said come back . . .!'

But Pete had gone.

44

As soon as the two policemen had gone Jem ran into the George and Dragon and yelled, 'Billy! Billy!'

'I'm over here, Jem,' came a small voice.

'Where?' Jem looked round wildly, fearing the policemen would come pounding back at any moment. 'Where are you?'

'Here.' A small hand appeared above the bar and waved at him.

Billy was sitting cross-legged on the floor, a half-eaten crusty roll in his hand. 'Ullo, Jem,' he grinned, his cheeks bulging. 'You been in a accident or some-thin'? You got blood all over you. Here,' he broke off a piece of the roll and offered it to his brother, 'you can have this, if you like. I've eaten three already. And I got a pork pie, a rattlin' good'un. It's got a chunk missin' cos a dog was eatin' it – look, you can see where its teeth went in – but there's a lot left,' he said, polishing the crust with his sleeve. 'Want a bit?'

'You little . . .! You mean you stayed behind just

to stuff your belly with bread and pork pie?' fumed Jem.

'Nah, I've eaten a lot of cheese too,' Billy grinned, well pleased with himself, 'and a jar of pickled onions and . . .'

'And I hope you're sick. Come on.' Jem yanked Billy to his feet. 'I haven't time to warm your backside now but I will, soon as we get . . . What was that?' He stopped, listening intently.

'What?' Billy paused in the middle of eating the rest of the roll.

'I thought I heard somethin'.'

'Must've been a rat. Some of them're still here. One tried to steal my cheese. I gave it a right whack on the nose and it—'

'Nah, it wasn't no rat. It was more like . . . Blimey!' Jem yelped. 'What's that?'

'Sounds like someone goin' down there,' whispered Billy, pointing to the stairs that led to the cellar.

The sound got louder and faster with every step until there was a crash at the bottom as if the person, if it was a person, had landed all of a heap.

'D'you think it's a crusher?' Billy said, his voice rising in alarm.

'Shh!' Jem slapped a hand over the little boy's

mouth. 'Follow me – and don't say nothin', don't make any noise, Billy, or I'll top you.'

Silently the two boys crawled out from behind the bar and looked fearfully around the room. A dozen or more rats were scuttling across the floor, stopping now and then to nibble the bits of food people had dropped in their haste to get away.

'Stay there a crack,' Jem breathed in Billy's ear and, crouching low, he moved stealthily to the top of the stairs.

'Oh, it's all right,' he said, relief flooding through him like a torrent of warm water, 'it was just a barrel.'

'A rat must've pushed it,' said Billy, running to look.

'One rat couldn't've pushed a barrel that size,' Jem frowned, his elation turning to alarm again. 'It'd take fifty, a hundred . . .'

'That's what did it,' Billy pointed as a terrier appeared at the foot of the stairs, looking up at them nervously.

Again Jem felt relief flooding through him. 'Come on, let's get out of here,' he said, running to the door. 'Ned's waitin' for us at . . . Hey up, what's wrong with this?' he said, tugging at the handle. 'Why won't the varminty thing open?'

'Cos of that,' said Billy, pointing to the bolt at the bottom.

'But I didn't bolt it,' said Jem, staring at it, perplexed.

'You must've,' said Billy, bending down and pulling it back.

'I didn't, I tell you.'

'Well open the door, Jem. Go on!' pleaded the little boy, struggling to reach the handle.

'I can't. It's locked.'

'Why'd you lock it?'

'I didn't!' Jem shouted in frustration. 'I keep tellin' you I didn't bolt it, I didn't lock it. Somebody else must've . . . Oh, Lor!' His pulse began to race as he realized what he'd said. 'Now listen to me careful, Billy.' He bent down and whispered in the little boy's ear. 'How many people did the crushers collar?'

'Don't know.' Billy shrugged.

'You do! Think!' insisted Jem, shaking him roughly. 'How many?'

Billy hesitated for a moment then he held up four fingers.

'Who were they?'

'Don't know.'

'Don't keep sayin' that.'

'There was that woman . . .'

'Nell,' Jem nodded. 'Who else?'

'An old fogey that looks like Gran, only worse.'

'That'd be Old Jack.'

'And Tom Ramsbum. He promised me eggs'n bacon, he did. And a pork pie and kippers and kidneys and—'

'Hold your jaw!' Jem hissed. 'Who else did the crushers collar? Who was the last one?'

'A man.'

'What was he like?' said Jem eagerly. 'Was his mouth kind've twisted right up his cheek like this?' He pulled a face. 'Did he have a couple of red holes where his nose should've been? Was he—?'

'Nah, his nose was like a beetroot, a big'un, and his belly . . .' Billy stretched his arms as far as he could to show the size of the man's girth.

'That'd be the landlord,' muttered Jem. 'That means they didn't catch the Terror. He's still around . . . somewhere.'

'D'you think he's here, Jem? D'you think he's still in this pub?'

'Nah,' Jem said without conviction.

'He is, isn't he?' said Billy in a small voice.

'Don't worry, he won't get us. We'll hide. Anyway, there're a couple of crushers outside . . .' But with a sinking heart Jem suddenly remembered

he'd sent the policemen on a wild goose chase. 'They'll be back in a moment and they'll . . .'

'. . . be too late,' said someone in a snuffling, whistling voice behind him.

Jem spun round. The Terror was standing in the middle of the room, hands on hips, leering at them.

'Jem, isn't it? And you must be Billy,' he said, as the two boys backed away from him, clutching each other. 'Got a good memory, haven't I? I don't forget nothin'. Oh no, not me. I don't forget that it was you that let all my rats out. I don't forget that it was cos of you the crushers collared my friends and would've collared me'n all if I hadn't hid.' He pointed to the panel in the wall that concealed the secret staircase to the rat pit.

'I . . . I . . .' began Jem, but he was so frightened his tongue had cleaved to the roof of his mouth and he could barely speak.

'Know what they'd do if they'd found me?' said the Terror. 'They'd string me up. Like that, wouldn't you?' His voice dropped to a hoarse whisper. 'Like to see me strung up, wouldn't you, Jem?'

'N . . . n . . . nah.'

'That's nice. That's very nice of you, very civilized.' The Terror grinned. 'But I got to say I don't feel the same about you, Jem,' he said, with mock sorrow.

'To tell you the truth, I want to see you and your pesky brother strung up. I can't wait to see it. That's why I got this.' He drew a length of rope from his pocket and dangled it in front of the boys. 'Just right, isn't it? It'll fit round your throats real nice, real snug, eh?'

'But . . . But we didn't do nothin'. We . . .'

'*Nothin'?*' roared the Terror. 'You call ruinin' my life, nothin'? See that?' He pointed to a wooden beam that stretched from one side of the room to the other, 'I'm goin' to hang you from that.'

Billy buried his head in Jem's coat, whimpering.

'It won't be a quick death,' the Terror gloated. 'I want you to contemplate all the trouble you've caused me. I want you to have plenty of time to think about it,' he chuckled, relishing the expression on the boys' faces. 'Now, which of you wants to go first? No offers? Well, let's start with the littl'un, shall we? We'll have a bit of fun watchin' him dance on the end of a rope, eh, Jem?'

Billy burst into tears. 'Don't let him, Jem,' he sobbed. 'Don't let him.'

'Let him go, mister. Please,' begged Jem. 'He's only . . .'

'*Let him go?*' scoffed the Terror. '*Let him go?* After all the trouble I've taken to . . .' he stopped, his eyes darting nervously to the door as someone pounded on it.

Jem's heart leaped – the crushers were back! – but the next moment he was cast into despair again as a familiar voice shouted, 'Jem! Jem! You in there?'

'Who is it?' hissed the Terror, hiding behind the door.

'P . . . Pete,' whispered Jem.

'And who's P . . . Pete?' the Terror mocked him.

'The kid that was with us – down there.'

'Oh, one of them useless brats.'

'Jem! Jem, let me in plaguy quick!' yelled Pete.

'All right, let him in before he breaks the bleedin' door down,' growled the Terror, tossing Jem the key. 'But don't do nothin' stupid, see, or . . .' He grabbed Billy by the hair and put a knife to his throat.

Jem put the key in the lock with trembling hands. This was his chance, probably his only chance to save himself and his brother. If he could warn Pete by a look, a wink – but he had barely opened the door before Pete barged in shouting, 'The Terror! Jem, they didn't get the Terror. He got away. He's . . .'

'. . . right here, just waitin' for you,' chuckled the Terror, kicking the door shut.

'Oh, blimey!' breathed Pete, his face ashen.

'Not pleased to see me, eh? Now that's a pity.' The

Terror chuckled again. 'Cos I'm real pleased to see you. Lock the door and give me the key,' he said to Jem.

Jem did as he was told, but in handing the key back to the Terror he pretended to fumble and it fell to the floor.

'Pick it up, you clumsy idiot!' the man screamed, his mood swinging from droll to demented in a flash, and as Jem bent down he cuffed him hard around the ears.

Seizing the opportunity Pete leaped at the Terror, but the man was too quick for him. Keeping a tight hold on Billy he lashed out at Pete, slamming him against the wall with such force that he slid to the floor, unconscious.

'Right, let's stop playin' games,' said the Terror. 'Get up on that.' He pointed to one of the tables that had managed to stay upright. 'Go on, both of you, get up there!'

His heart pounding so hard he thought it would break through his ribs, Jem stumbled on to the table, pulling Billy with him.

'Guv, please . . .' he pleaded.

'Shut up!' snarled the Terror, throwing the rope at him. 'Put this round his neck.'

'I can't! I can't!'

'Well, you got a choice, son,' the Terror purred. 'You can put the rope round his neck and string him up or —' He caressed the knife lovingly — 'I'll cut him up *very slowly*, startin' with his toes and workin' up till I get to his—'

'Nah!' shrieked Billy.

'So what's it to be?' The Terror leered at Jem.

Pete's eyes opened, closed and flickered open again. For a moment he didn't know where he was. What he did know was that his head felt as if it had been kicked up and down the street several times and blood was trickling from his nose. He sat up, blinking. Then he saw Jem, staring at him over the Terror's shoulder, his eyes wide with fear.

Pete glanced at the door — if only he could open it, if only he could get out and . . . His heart did a double somersault. The key was still on the floor where Jem had dropped it. With a warning nod to Jem he slunk down on his belly and slowly, scarcely breathing, inched his way towards it.

The Terror half turned, as if he sensed the boy snaking across the floor behind him, but to distract him Jem gave Billy a violent shove that shot him right off the table. 'Run, Billy!' he shouted at him. 'Run!'

'He's not runnin' nowhere,' growled the Terror, grabbing Billy.

Pete had almost reached the key . . .

Billy struggled, flailing at the Terror with fists and feet, but the man shook him till his teeth rattled and hurled him back on to the table.

Pete stretched out his hand and closed his fingers around the key . . .

'Tie that rope round his neck. NOW!' the Terror screamed at Jem.

Pete stood up and put the key in the lock . . .

'Now loop it round that beam . . . Not that one, you stupe. The one above your head.'

Pete turned the key in the lock and was about to open the door when a man burst in, knocking him flat on his back.

'Pa!' shouted Jem.

His father took in the situation at a glance and bellowing with rage he lunged at the Terror. The man was momentarily thrown off his guard but he quickly regained control and brandishing his knife he hissed, 'Don't come no closer or I'll . . . Aaargh!' He staggered back as Jem's boot connected with his head.

'That's the ticket, Jem!' cried Pa, and he slammed his huge fist into the man's face, sending him flying

over the bar where he landed with another 'Aaargh!' and lay silent.

'Billy!' Pa's eyes lit up as the little boy hurled himself into his arms. 'Lor', love a duck, your ma'll be so pleased to see you, son. And so am I – though I could toe your backside for all the grief you put us through, straight I could . . . Nice work, Jem,' he said, putting his arm around Jem's shoulders. 'We make a good team, we do. We . . . Oh, damnation,' he groaned as two constables came running into the saloon, spinning their rattles, 'now we're in for it.'

45

'What'll we do now?' said Ned disconsolately. 'Pete's been gone a dog's age.'

'Scarper, like Jem said.'

'But we can't just leave him and Billy and Pete.'

'I wasn't sayin' we would,' retorted Clem hotly. 'I was sayin' we'd go home and get help and come back and . . . Oy, here comes a police cart. Goin' like a dose of salts too.'

'And the Terror's in it,' cried Ned, catching sight of the man's hideous face as the horses galloped by. 'They got him! They got him! And . . . Lawks a mercy, they got my pa too. And my brothers.'

'And they got Pete,' said Clem, her eyes filling with tears. 'The crushers've copped the lot.'

46

Although Billy slept soundly, Jem and Pete had a miserable night in the police cells, mainly because Pa moaned on and on about the injustice of it all.

'We done nothin' wrong, nah, nothin' at all, but it don't make no difference. They're always down on the likes of us whether we done somethin' wrong or not. Now if we were toffs . . . Ah, that'd be different. It'd be, "Sorry, Your Lordship, our mistake, Your Lordship, we wouldn't dream of blamin' you, Your Lordship, just cos you topped your wife and kids and robbed your neighbours blind." But the workin' man's trampled on. He's got no rights, he gets no respect, no justice. Look at me, innocent as a newborn baby, but they'll still put me in clink, you see. Oh yeh, they'll put me away for many a year. And for why? I ask you, for—?'

'Pa,' muttered Jem.

'What is it, son?'

'Shut up, will you, I'm tryin' to sleep.'

47

The following morning Pa and the boys were brought before the magistrate, a stern man who peered at them over metal-rimmed spectacles.

'Of what are they accused?' he asked.

'Your Honour, they are all accomplices of Jim Rippen,' said the clerk of the court. 'They were caught red-handed at the scene of the crime by—'

'It's a bleedin' lie!' cried Pa. 'I wasn't no 'complice. I just went to the George'n Dragon to get my kids back cos the Terror'd—'

'Hold your tongue!' the clerk scolded him. 'And address His Honour as "Your Honour". Better still, don't address him at all.'

'But I'm innocent, you stupid bugger! So are my kids. They were grabbed by the Terror and—'

'Mr Perkins . . .' the magistrate interrupted him.

'Perkin*ski*,' said Pa.

'Mr Perkinski, I suggest you calm down and tell

the court what occurred — *without expletives*,' he said sternly.

'Without what?' said Pa.

'Swear words,' explained the clerk.

'Oh right. Well, it was like this, guv — Your Honour . . .' Pa took a deep breath and explained what had happened . . . 'And then Jem gave the Terror a clout in the loft,' he concluded, 'and I gave him a right stockdollager in the kisser.'

'They gave him what?' The magistrate leaned towards the clerk, frowning.

'A kick in the head and a punch in the mouth, Your Honour.'

'I see. And as a result of the "right stockdollager" I presume the man was severely incapacitated, Mr Perkinski?'

'Severe what?'

'He came a cropper,' said the clerk.

'Oh yeh, he did, Your Honour. He went out like a light.'

'Which resulted in his apprehension?' said the magistrate.

'His what?' said Pa.

'He was copped,' said the clerk.

'What's the matter with the beak?' Pa hissed at him. 'Don't he speak English?'

'His Honour speaks perfectly good English, Mr Perkinski. It is you who—'

'Yes, yes, never mind all that,' said the magistrate. 'What is the reward for the capture of this villain?'

'Here, I'm no villain!' protested Pa.

'I was referring to Jim Rippen, Mr Perkinski.'

'Who?'

'The Terror,' said the clerk.

'Oh, right,' said Pa.

'There is no reward, Your Honour,' said the clerk, looking puzzled, 'since the guilty party has already been apprehended.'

'Tut, tut, man,' said the magistrate testily. 'I meant what would the reward have been if the guilty party had not yet been apprehended?'

'Five guineas, Your Honour.'

'Hmm . . .' The magistrate stroked his chin thoughtfully. 'Well, in view of the notoriety of this dangerous criminal and the bravery of Mr Perkinski and his sons in assisting in his arrest . . .'

'And me,' piped up Pete. 'I opened the door so this old fogey could get in.'

'Here, who you callin' an old fogey?' cried Pa.

'Silence in court!' shouted the clerk, as Pa and Pete squared up to each other.

'In view of the bravery of you *all*,' continued the magistrate, 'I am awarding you five guineas.'

'Five guineas?' exclaimed Pa.

'Just so, Mr Perkinski.'

'Five guineas . . .' Pa shook his head as if he couldn't quite believe it. 'Well, Your Honour, I've said it before and I'll say it again, the British justice system's the finest in the world. Don't matter if you're a toff or a workin' man, rich or poor,' he declaimed, stressing every word with a nod of the head, 'you're all treated the same in this great country of ours, you're treated fair and square. You got rights, you get respect, you get justice, you get—'

'Yes, yes, thank you, Mr Perkinski,' said the magistrate, wincing. 'Get him out,' he muttered to the clerk of the court, 'plaguy quick!'

48

Mr Bullock, Clem, Alfie and Ned were waiting outside the court when Pa appeared with the boys, grinning and clapping each other on the back.

'Pete!' cried Clem, throwing her arms around his neck.

'We got off, Clem,' he said, swinging her round and round. 'We're free!'

'You shouldn't have got yourself mixed up with them lot in the first place,' snapped Mr Bullock, nodding at Pa and his sons.

'Oh?' Pa bridled. 'And who might you be?'

'The name's Bullock. George to my friends, mister to you. Sweepmaster to the gentry.'

'So you're the scoundrel that nabbed my son?' growled Pa, clenching his fists.

'Nabbed?' cried Mr Bullock.

'Nabbed!' shouted Pa, his face turning puce.

'I *nabbed* him? I like that, I really do. I find this poor

little kid runnin' around in the fog, cryin' cos he's lost and . . .'

'That right, Jem?' Pa turned to him.

'Well, Pa, like I told you, Billy was dawdlin' along and . . .'

'How the hell would he know?' bawled Mr Bullock. 'He's the one that lost him. Should've looked after his little brother 'stead of walkin' away and leavin' him for me to find. So what did I do?' he shouted down Jem's protests. 'Did I leave the poor little mite in the fog, cold and hungry, cryin' his eyes out? I should've done, I realize now I should've done,' he said indignantly, ''stead of takin' him into my own home and givin' him a nice warm bed to sleep in and plenty of hot, nourishin' food and work to do so's he could learn how to make a livin' for himself . . . Nah, there's no need to thank me, son,' he said as Billy tried to interrupt him. 'I'd have done it for any poor little kid. That's the kind of bloke I am.'

'Well,' Pa looked confused, to say the least, 'I didn't realize . . .'

'Nah, you didn't,' snapped Mr Bullock. 'But I accept your apology and Pete's share of the reward.'

'Reward?'

'What the beak gave you for coppin' the Terror.'

'Oh . . . Oh, that reward. Yeh, well, it was just a small one, very small, a couple of quid I think it was.'

'Five.'

'Five, was it?'

'Guineas.' Mr Bullock held out his hand.

Pa took it in his and shook it.

'I want Pete's share,' snapped Mr Bullock, freeing himself from Pa's firm grip.

'Oh . . . Oh, right,' said Pa. And grudgingly he put some money in the sweepmaster's outstretched hand.

'Let's go home now, Dad,' said Clem, linking her arm through Pete's. 'Come on, Alfie.'

'Nah.' Mr Bullock shook his head. 'I don't want that little runt. He's no use to me.'

'But, Dad . . .'

'Clem, I can't feed and clothe all the orphans in London.'

'I'm not a orphan,' protested Alfie. 'I live with my father.'

'Where's that?' asked Clem.

'Nowhere.'

'What d'you mean nowhere?'

'We never live in a proper home. We live in lodgin' houses all over the place. But I think I could find Dad if somebody was to help me,' Alfie said hopefully.

'What's he do?' asked Pa.

'Sells cakes from his tray.'

'Where?'

'Trafalgar Square, mostly.'

'The Square? Your pa isn't Nobby Clark by any chance, is he?'

'Yeh, that's him.' Alfie ran to Pa, looking up at him eagerly. 'D'you know him, mister?'

'Know him?' Pa chuckled. 'I'd say I do. Him and me were in clink together years ago. We'll have no trouble findin' old Nobby.'

'Can we go now, mister? Can we?'

'Nah, son, I'm too done up. But we'll go in the mornin' – and that's a promise.'

49

Ma was so overjoyed to see Billy she burst into tears, gave him a resounding wallop that set him bawling and hugged him to her. 'It's good to have you back again, my tulip,' she said, rocking him in her arms.

'And we got a reward, Ma,' said Jem proudly.

'Four guineas,' said Pa, putting the money in her hand.

'I'll be jiggered,' she exclaimed, looking at it in amazement. 'I never had that much money in my life.'

'What'll we do with it?' said Ned.

'I want a pork pie, want a pork pie,' cried Billy, jumping up and down excitedly.

'I'm not wastin' a penny of it on tomfoolery,' said Ma sternly. 'Pa needs a new jacket. You look a sight in them trousers, Jem. Ned could do with a shirt. Gran's got more holes than leather in her boots. And as for this . . .' She took off her brimless boater and tossed it into a corner.

'But a pork pie isn't tomfoolery,' said Jem aghast. 'It's grub.'

'Please, Ma,' pleaded Billy, threatening to start crying again.

'Oh, all right,' she conceded. 'Just one.'

'Each,' said Jem.

Ma began to protest but Pa cut in quickly, 'Yeh, one each.'

'And me, mister?' Alfie tugged at his sleeve. 'Can I have one?'

'Course you can,' Pa laughed. 'Go on, Jem, up to the cookshop with you. Give him the money, Ma.'

With some reluctance Ma put a shilling in Jem's hand.

'Oh, and son,' she said as he turned to go. 'I want the change.' She narrowed her eyes at him. '*All* of it.'

A Note from the Author

James Cannon

'Jim Rippen, the Walworth Terror' is loosely based on James Cannon, the Walworth Terror, a mid-nineteenth-century sweepmaster who was notorious for his cruelty. He had seventeen convictions for assault in ten years. Finally he was arrested for attacking two policemen and sentenced to two years in prison for injuring one of them, but the case was transferred to the Old Bailey, where a jury found him guilty on the capital charge of attempting to murder the other policeman. He was condemned to hang, but the punishment was changed to penal servitude and the Walworth Terror was shipped to Australia to end his days there. Well, I assume he ended his days there. Then again he might have swum back . . .

Jack Black

'Old Jack' was inspired by Jack Black, who was Queen Victoria's rat and mole destroyer. He started his 'career' at the age of nine at a Mr Strickland's cow farm in Regent's Park, but soon found that selling rats for the rat-and-dog sport was more profitable. Despite being so severely bitten that his wounds turned septic and two or three times he was close to death, Jack was never afraid of handling rats and seemed to have a genuine affection and respect for them.

When he gave up rat (and practically every other small animal, bird and insect) catching, he bought a pub, but this business enterprise eventually went bust and he had to leave London. Clearly Jack would have been better off with the Walworth Terror.

Jack Sheppard

Although many poor London children had never heard of Queen Victoria they knew all about Jack Sheppard, a notorious thief who escaped from prison so many times he became a hero. Born in Spitalfields in 1702 he grew up in the Bishopsgate workhouse and was apprenticed to a carpenter. He broke free of his apprenticeship after six years and turned to thieving as his livelihood and was caught and imprisoned six times. The fifth time he was chained to the floor in Newgate Prison, his legs secured with irons and his hands cuffed, but somehow he managed to slip his hands through the handcuffs, loosen one of the links in the chains about his legs with a small nail and squeeze through the great chains around his body. He was recaptured and taken to court, surrounded by a huge number of admirers, and sentenced to hang at Tyburn.

A Glossary of Victorian Slang and Phrases

Neither Jem, Ned, Billy or the author made up any of the words or expressions in this book, even the golopshus ones. They were all part of common speech in Victorian times.

All-overish	Neither sick nor well
Area	Small space in front of the basement of a house
Argufy	Argue
Article	Person
Beak	Magistrate
Bowlas	Tarts made of bread, apple and sugar
Bracelets	Handcuffs
Carriage and pair	Carriage and two (usually matching in size and colour) horses
Chonkeys	Mincemeat baked in a crust
Clack	Chatter
Collywobbles	Stomach ache
Combinations	Vest and long underpants all in one garment
Come a mucker	To come to grief
Coventries	Three-cornered jam puffs
Crack	Excellent. Also 'in a crack' — in a moment
Crimes!	Exclamation of dismay
Croodle	Nestle close together
Devil-dodger	Clergyman
Dipper	Pickpocket
Dot and Carry One	Person with a wooden leg. The 'dot' is

	the impression made by the wooden leg while the good leg is 'carried'
Dressed up to the knocker	Very well dressed
Drop off the hook	Die
Duffer	Slow-witted person
Fly	Clever/artful
Game	Crippled/wounded
Gardy loo!	'Gardez l'eau!' is French for 'Watch out for the water!' This is where our word 'loo' comes from
Giffle-gaffle	Nonsense
Glump	Sulk
Go like one o'clock	Move very fast
Golopshus	Delicious
Growler	Four-wheeled, horse-drawn cab
Gull	Someone who is easily tricked. Also to trick someone
Hansom cab	Light two-wheeled, horse-drawn cab
Honour bright	Word of honour
Hornswoggle	Nonsense
Howsomever	However
In the attic	In the head
In the loft	In the head
Jammy	Wonderful/lucky/profitable
Judy	Woman
Jumbles	Thin, crisp cakes made of flour, butter and treacle
Lawks/Lor'	Lord
Leary	Clever/artful
Love a duck	Exclamation of surprise or pleasure
Moll	Woman

Needful	Money
Pawnshop	Place where one can leave an object as security for money lent by a pawnbroker
Pea-souper	Thick yellow fog
Plaguy	Very
Plummy	Excellent
Pool of London	Stretch of the Thames between London Bridge and the Tower, which was crammed with every kind of vessel
Porter	Bitter, dark-brown beer originally brewed for porters
Queer in the attic	Mentally impaired
Ready	Money
Scarify	Scare
Shindy	Commotion
Slantingdicular	Slanted, as opposed to perpendicular
Snaggy	Irritable
Spats	Cloth or leather covering to protect shoes
Splendiferous	Splendid
Spooney	In love
Square	Good/honest
Stash it!	Shut up!
Stow it!	Shut up!
Stupe	Stupid person
Treadmill	Treadmills were small, closed compartments in which men were imprisoned for fifteen minutes at a time, treading down a wheel of

twenty-four steps at a fixed speed. As the steps were always sinking away from under their feet the prisoners could get no firm tread, which made it exhausting

Varmint	Naughty child/rascal
Whacker	Lie
Whim-wham	Nonsense
Whopper	Lie
Wideawake	Hat with a wide brim and shallow crown

Up until 1971 these were the notes and coins used in Britain. When decimal currency was introduced in 1971, a shilling became the new five-pence piece.

A farthing/a fadge	One quarter of a penny
A halfpenny/a ha'penny	One half of a penny
A penny	One penny
Two pennies/tuppence	Two pence
Three pennies/thrups	Three pence, a threepenny bit
Six pennies/a tanner	Six pence
Twelve pennies	One shilling
Two shillings	A florin
Two shillings and six pence/half a wheel	Half a crown
Five shillings/a cartwheel	A crown
Ten shillings/ten bob/half a quid	Ten shillings
Twenty shillings/a quid	One pound, a sovereign
Twenty-one shillings/a ned	A guinea

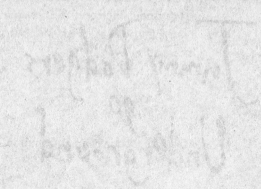

Look out for the following title from
Macmillan Children's Books

Jammy Dodgers go Underground

by Bowering Sivers

Jem, Ned and Billy are the Jammy Dodgers — three boys who pride themselves on being able to beg, borrow or blag their way out of a tight spot. The Perkinski brothers can slide out of trouble as smoothly as a jellied eel, and always land jammy side up.

Except for the fateful night when, down on their luck, far from home and without as much as a dry crust of bread in their bellies, the boys take a wrong turn — and wind up locked away in the workhouse under the evil eye of its brutal master, George Blood. But the Jammy Dodgers aren't easily beaten, and where there's a will there's a way out . . . But as escape routes go though, this one stinks.

Venture deep down into the labyrinths of London in JAMMY DODGERS GO UNDERGROUND. Dark, dirty and dangerous — not everyone gets out alive.